IN ROMANCE

Christmas in Romance, Book 1
by
***USA Today* Bestselling Author**
SHANNA HATFIELD

Sleigh Bells Ring in Romance
(Christmas in Romance, Book 1)

Copyright © 2018 by Shanna Hatfield

ISBN: 9781729037416

All rights reserved. By purchasing this publication through an authorized outlet, you have been granted the nonexclusive, nontransferable right to access and read the text of this ebook in a digital format. No part of this publication may be reproduced, distributed, downloaded, decompiled, reverse engineered, transmitted, or stored in or introduced into any information storage and retrieval system, in any form or by any means, including photocopying, recording, or other electronic or mechanical methods, now known or hereafter invented, without the written permission of the author, except in the case of brief quotations embodied in reviews and certain other noncommercial uses permitted by copyright law. Please purchase only authorized editions.

For permission requests, please contact the author, with a subject line of "permission request" at the e-mail address below or through her website.
Shanna Hatfield
shanna@shannahatfield.com
shannahatfield.com

This is a work of fiction. Names, characters, businesses, places, events, and incidents either are the product of the author's imagination or are used in a fictitious manner. Any resemblance to actual persons, living or dead, business establishments, or actual events is purely coincidental.

Cover Design by Shanna Hatfield

To Mom and Dad...
thank you for your wonderful example
of long-lasting and true love.

.

Books by Shanna Hatfield

FICTION

Prologue

"Did he see you sneak out here?" Blayne Grundy asked, peering around the edge of the barn door as he lingered in the shadows.

Janet Moore shook her head and tugged her sweater more closely around her in the nippy November air. "No. Dad is zonked out taking a nap. He's been exhausted since he came home from the hospital. Who would have thought the mighty Jess Milne would sleep more than a toddler after having knee replacement surgery? At least the doctor said he's doing well and should have a normal recovery." She stepped out of view of anyone passing by, moving closer to Blayne. "I never thought we'd resort to holding a clandestine meeting in the barn to discuss the love life, or lack thereof, of my dad and your grandmother."

Blayne chuckled and leaned against the wall behind him, crossing his arms over his broad chest.

"Honestly, it's never something I envisioned, either. It's nice of you to use your vacation time to come take care of your dad while he heals. How long are you planning to stay before you fly back to Salt Lake City?"

"Until the first of December, but then I have to get back home. By that time, Steve and the kids will either have learned how to take care of themselves or be living off pizza and take-out food while dressed in filthy clothes. I'm not convinced any of them know how to turn on the washing machine."

He smirked then tossed her a cocky smile. "You know I had a huge crush on you when you used to babysit me."

Janet nodded. "Since you followed me around like a besotted puppy, I was aware of that fact."

"I did no such thing," Blayne said, scowling at the woman who had been his neighbor, babysitter, and was now a good friend.

"You did and you know it," Janet pinned him with a perceptive glare. "But let's figure out what to do about Dad and your grandmother. Do you have any idea why Doris refuses to speak to him?"

"Not a clue. She isn't the least bit helpful when I've asked her why she turns all lemon-faced at the very mention of Jess." Blayne sighed, removed his dusty cowboy hat, and forked a hand through his hair. "I've done everything I can think of to get those two together. It's obvious to everyone but Jess and Grams that they should fall in love."

"The problem is that they are both too stubborn and opinionated to admit they like each other. We'll just have to get creative." Janet plopped down on a bale of straw. When one of the ranch dogs wandered inside, she absently reached down and rubbed behind his ears. She glanced up at Blayne. "What does your wife think about all this?"

"Brooke is all for whatever makes Grams happy, and Jess, too. She and your dad get along like old friends."

"I'm glad to hear that. Brooke is fantastic, Blayne. You couldn't have found a better girl to marry."

Blayne's face softened at the mention of his wife. "She is pretty special."

Janet remained silent for several moments, lost in thought, before she looked up at Blayne with a confident smile. "What if I suddenly had to return home and no one else could stay with Dad? Could you persuade Doris to take care of him until he's back on his feet? If they had to see each other every day for two or three weeks, maybe they'd get past whatever it is that's keeping them apart."

A slow, pleased grin spread across Blayne's face. "I think, with enough guilt, it might work. I can remind Grams of the number of times she'd lectured me about it being not just a duty, but an honor and privilege to help take care of our friends and neighbors in times of need."

"Perfect! I'll see if I can get on a flight tomorrow. If not, the next day at the latest. Steve is going to be thrilled at this bit of news." Janet hopped up and tugged her cell phone from her pocket. "I just hope our plan works. Doris and Dad have too many good years left for them to spend the time alone."

"Especially when they clearly would like to be together." Blayne pushed away from the wall. "With a little holiday magic, anything is possible."

Janet nodded in agreement. "It certainly is…"

Chapter One

"Consider yourself officially disowned, effective immediately."

The shocked expression Doris Grundy expected from her grandson never materialized. He didn't even bother to appear disturbed by her announcement. Instead, the cheeky rascal had the audacity to laugh at her.

With a harsh scowl, she reached for the plate holding a large wedge of warm apple pie she'd placed in front of him only moments earlier, before he stirred her anger.

Blayne grabbed the dish before she could snatch it away and held it beyond her grasp. "You aren't gonna disown me, Grams. You should find a new threat since you haven't followed through on that one the past fifty times you've used it."

"I haven't threatened you fifty times, Blayne,

and you know it. But I should follow through this time. How dare you?" Doris fisted her hands on her hips and glared at him as he held the plate close to his face and hurriedly shoveled pie into his mouth.

Although he currently acted like a misbehaving child, it was hard for her to believe Blayne was a full-grown man with a beautiful wife. He and Brooke had married not quite a year ago. He'd been running the family ranch near the town of Romance, Oregon, since he graduated from college, proving himself as a responsible, capable adult.

Yet, part of her longed for him to be the little boy who used to curl up beside her and beg for a bedtime story. In place of that adorable imp she'd loved from the first moment she'd held him in her arms, her grandson was now a strapping man.

Without a thought to the bushels of trouble it would cause her, Blayne had volunteered her to help their neighbor while he recuperated from knee-replacement surgery. Jess Milne had been a widower for six years and had expressed his yearning for her to become his next wife. Doris had no interest in remarrying, especially not *that* man.

"How could you do this to me?" she asked, wanting to knock the smirk off Blayne's handsome face.

Blayne quickly shoved the last bite of pie in his mouth and carried the dish to the sink before he leaned against the counter and crossed his arms over his broad chest. "Why are you acting as cross as a cat with its tail shut in the door? I think the lady doth protest too much because she really likes Jess."

Her scowl shifted into a glower. "I'm not acting

like an out-of-sorts cat," she snapped. "And I'm not protesting too much, you smart-alecky upstart. I just have better things to do with my time than kowtowing to that old coot. Why can't his daughter take care of him?"

Blayne continued smiling in that infuriating, knowing way he inherited directly from her, which made it all the more annoying. "Because Janet has to return to Salt Lake City, Grams. She already took a week and a half off work and needs to get back. Besides, her kids are involved in sports and one of them is in the state playoffs."

"I don't see why that senile old goat couldn't schedule his surgery at a better time. Next week is Thanksgiving, after all." Doris glanced at the calendar, thinking of all the preparations she needed to see to before the holiday. "Janet should have at least stayed through Thanksgiving."

"Grams, are you even listening to a word I say?" Blayne rolled his eyes and took a step toward her. "Janet stayed as long as she could. What's she supposed to do about work and her family?"

Doris had no answer because Blayne was right. However, it didn't change the fact he'd volunteered her help without even asking her first.

"Come on, Grams. It's not like you have to do it forever, just a few weeks. Brooke said she'd help when she's not at Blown Away. You know she can't be gone from her shop too much this time of year. She gets a lot of orders for custom blown glass pieces for the holidays." Blayne settled his hands on her shoulders and looked at her with an intense sapphire blue gaze so like her own. "It's not like you to be this way. Usually you're the first one to offer a hand when someone needs it. Jess will be all alone over there when Janet leaves. From what I saw, he's having quite a time getting around. If it was anyone but him, you'd be over there doing everything you could to help."

Assailed with guilt, Doris tried to ignore it but found she couldn't. Not when it pricked so uncomfortably at her conscience. "Fine, but as soon as December arrives, that hairy-eared baboon is on his own."

Blayne looked like he worked to subdue a grin, but he nodded once then pulled her to him, giving her a warm hug. "That's my girl."

Doris snuggled against him, inhaling the scent of leather and horses clinging to his flannel shirt. "I thought I'd been relegated to second best girl status and was no longer up for cuddles like this."

A chuckle rolled out of her grandson and he kissed the top of her head. "You wouldn't expect anyone to hold the number one spot other than my wife, would you?"

"Of course not, sweetie," Doris said.

"You'll always be near the top of my list, though, Grams."

"I'm glad for that." She patted his cheek, seeing so much of his father and grandfather in his face. For a moment, the resemblance caused an aching pain to pierce her heart. "Now get out of here and back to work. If I have to begin my sentence over at Happy Hearts Ranch tomorrow, I've got a lot of work to do."

Blayne stepped back with a look of concern. "I

didn't mean to make more work for you. It wasn't my intention."

She pinched his cheek, aware of how much he pretended to hate it. "I know, honey. You men are clueless when it comes to what is involved with giving care, especially to a lunkheaded dolt like Jess Milne."

Blayne's grin returned. "I'm glad to hear you still hold him in such high regard. Someday, you're gonna have to tell me what he did to get on your bad side."

"That's none of your business. Now scoot or I'll put you to work plucking a chicken."

He snagged his hat and coat from the hooks set in the wall and yanked open the door. "See you at dinner, Grams."

She smiled as she watched him settle the hat on his head and jog down the back porch steps. His long legs quickly carried him across the yard as he headed toward the barn, with the ranch dogs racing around him.

Despite how much Blayne had irked her, she was proud of the good, strong, kindhearted man he'd grown into. It was his thoughtful, giving nature that had put her in the terrible position of helping out their neighbor.

"I'll get that boy back, but good," Doris muttered as she took out her mixing bowl and set to work making a batch of cookies.

Chapter Two

"You did what?" Jess Milne bellowed as his daughter picked up the tray she'd set across his lap with his lunch.

"You heard me, Dad," Janet said, turning away and marching into the kitchen with the empty dishes.

Jess managed to grab his walker and move it in front of his chair then carefully pull himself upright. Unsteady but unwilling to ask for help, he followed Janet into the kitchen.

"Why can't you stay?" Jess asked, mindful not to raise his voice as he spoke.

Janet looked at him as he took a seat at the kitchen table with a painful grunt. She placed the plate she held into the dishwasher, rinsed her hands, and then walked over to the table.

"I've told you, Dad, I'm out of vacation time

and I have to get home. Marc is competing in the state playoffs this weekend, and I'd hate to miss that. Mallory needs help with a big school project. Besides, Steve has probably left a pile of laundry sky-high for me to take care of. I swear that man pretends to be stupid when it comes to turning on the washing machine. If I don't tackle the dirty clothes soon, they'll overtake the house. I'll have to dress my husband and kids in bed sheets, because I know they won't have bothered to change their beds while I'm gone. The spare sheets in the linen closet will be the only clean things in the house."

Jess studied his daughter with pain pinching his heart. She looked so much like his beloved wife. Julia had passed away more than six years ago due to respiratory failure, but sometimes his heart ached like he'd lost her just yesterday. When he and Julia had wed right out of high school, they planned to have half a dozen kids. Years went by with no children, then Janet had arrived quite unexpectedly the year he'd turned forty.

Determined she not become spoiled as an only child, they'd taught her to work hard, be self-reliant and independent, yet tempered her drive to succeed with lessons in generosity, love, and tenderness.

Janet had grown into a lovely, caring, successful woman of whom he was generally quite proud. However, she'd gone a step too far today.

"But why did you arrange for *her* to come help me? Why can't Blayne do it?" Jess asked, ignoring the fact he sounded like a whiny boy instead of a man nearing octogenarian status.

An exasperated sigh rolled out of his daughter.

"If you're referring to Doris Grundy, she seemed the most sensible candidate for the job. Blayne's far too busy with the ranch to run over here several times a day to check on you. And before you ask about his wife, you know she's got her hands full with the blown glass shop in town."

"I still don't know why an artist like Brooke would decide to move to a town like Romance." Jess flicked away a crumb from the tablecloth, one he'd probably left there when Janet insisted he eat breakfast at the table.

"Romance is a wonderful town, friendly and welcoming. Why wouldn't she want to stay here? Besides, from what I heard, it didn't take long for Blayne to turn her head." Janet grinned at him. "Or maybe it was the fact he liked her pigs that won her heart."

Jess chuckled. "Brooke is crazy about her pigs. You ought to see the way the three of them follow her around at the ranch."

"And what about you?" Janet lifted an eyebrow and pointed out the window toward the barn. "What in the world are you going to do with that little piglet out in the barn? Paint pink flowers on the stall door or maybe tie a little satin bow on her tail?"

Jess growled at her. "I plan to enjoy many pieces of crispy, perfectly cooked homegrown bacon."

Janet shook her head. "You can't fool me, Dad. You might have started out planning to raise that piglet for meat, but once you named her Pigtails, the solitary reason you'd eat her is if she was the only thing between you and complete starvation."

"Oh, what do you know?" Jess asked, annoyed his daughter knew him so well. He sat back and glowered at her. "So when is the wicked witch scheduled to fly over on her broom?"

"Dad!" Janet chided. "Doris Grundy is a kind, wonderful, sweet woman. What is it about her that rubs you the wrong way? I thought you liked her. You and Mom used to be such good friends with the Grundy family."

Jess shrugged, feigning indifference. He'd never admit it to anyone, least of all his bossy, albeit well-meaning daughter, but that sharp-tongued woman had hurt him.

He and Julia had lived just down the road from Glen and Doris Grundy for almost fifty years. They'd been close friends, shared many meals together, and attended church together. When Glen and Doris lost their only son and daughter-in-law in a plane crash, he and Julia had been the first to go over to offer comfort and help. Doris and Glen had already been raising Blayne since his folks were caught up in the world of corporate travel, but the boy was only eight when his parents died.

Jess had been there ten years ago when Glen died so unexpectedly of a heart attack. Julia had spent hours with Doris, supporting her through her grief while Jess did what he could to assist on the ranch until Blayne finished his last few months of college and graduated. The young man came home every chance he could to help and would have dropped out of school, but Jess and Julia, along with Doris, had insisted he graduate since he was so close to earning his bachelor's degree in agribusiness.

Then, when Julia passed away, Doris had been there with enough casseroles to fill his freezer for a month and comforting words of sympathy and understanding. She assured him the gaping hole in his heart and life wouldn't always hurt so badly, and he'd eventually come out on the other side of his grief.

For the first year after Julia's death, Jess hadn't wanted to go on, but he had. One day, he'd awakened and the weight of his grief had lessened. It took another year before he felt like he could breathe normally again. It was the third year after Julia had passed away that he'd looked up at a branding over at the Rockin' G Ranch and watched Doris laugh at something one of the ranch hands had said. That day, he saw her not as a nice neighbor he'd known most of his life, but a lovely woman he'd like to get to know as more than a friend.

It took another six months for him to get past the feeling he was cheating on not only Julia, but Glen. He'd loved his wife with his whole heart, but he finally realized she wouldn't want him to be alone, to be lonely. And Glen wouldn't want Doris to be that way either. Glen had been a great friend to him, and Jess would never have done anything to mar that friendship. But a part of him felt he had Glen's approval for his interest in Doris.

He hadn't gone courting since he was eighteen and had no idea how to go about it. Maybe he'd bungled things in his attempts to woo Doris. He'd tried talking her into accompanying him to events in

Romance, but she refused. He'd offered to drive her to Portland for dinner or a show, but she was always busy. Last Thanksgiving, he'd even purchased one of Brooke's blown glass vases and had the local florist fill it with a seasonal arrangement. Doris thanked him, but not with the enthusiasm he anticipated she'd exhibit.

Then in February, he'd asked her to go with him to a Valentine dance. Convinced she'd go, he'd pinned all his hopes on finally making headway in claiming Doris's heart. She'd turned him down flatter than a tire full of nails and made it clear, in no uncertain terms, she had no interest in dating him. Not then and not ever.

Rebuffed and angry, he may have said a few things he shouldn't have. She lambasted him until both his ears burned. He tossed the bouquet of roses he'd brought her on the ground and stormed off. The two of them had barely spoken more than a dozen words since then, even though they attended the same church, shopped at the same stores, and often saw each other in passing on the road.

And now his busybody daughter had arranged for Doris to keep an eye on him while he recuperated from his surgery. He should have listened to Janet in the first place and gone to Salt Lake City to have the knee-replacement done where he could have recuperated at her house.

But he'd never spent more than a week away from the ranch, and that was only when Julia insisted they take a vacation in the cold, dreary month of January. He couldn't be gone for the six weeks his doctor told him his recovery would take.

Although he was basically stuck in the house for a few weeks, he could still watch out the windows and pass orders down to his ranch hands. The foreman checked in each morning and evening, keeping him apprised of what was happening on the ranch.

"Dad?" Janet settled her hand over his and gave him an imploring look. "I thought you and Doris were friends. She was so good to us when Mom passed away. I remember going to the Rockin' G all the time when I was a kid. When I was in school, babysitting Blayne was a lucrative source of employment. What happened between you two?"

Jess smiled and settled his other hand on top of Janet's, patting it gently. Resigned to the inevitable, he released a sigh. "I don't suppose anything I say will change your mind about leaving in the morning?"

"No, Dad. I really do need to get home. I miss my husband and kids, even if all they keep me around for is to feed them, organize their social engagements, and make sure they have clean underwear."

Jess laughed. "Oh, I think they like you for more than those reasons." His laughter faded and he squeezed her fingers. "I appreciate the time you've spent with me, Janet. Thank you for coming."

"Of course, Dad. I'm just sorry I can't stay longer. Next time you have a long recovery ahead of you, will you please think about coming to Salt Lake City? You know we'd love to have you stay with us."

"Yes, I will." He smiled at her. "How are you

getting to the airport? Do I need to have one of the boys drive you?"

"No, Brooke Grundy is going to take me. She has a custom order to deliver to a hotel in downtown Portland and said she wouldn't mind dropping me off at the airport."

"Those interfering Grundy's again," he grumbled.

Janet pretended she didn't hear him as she rose to her feet. She kissed his cheek. "Why don't you rest while I put a roast on for dinner and write down a list of things Doris will need to know about your care?"

Jess winced at the mention of Doris's name, but nodded his head and slowly returned to his recliner. After settling into it, he leaned back, closed his eyes, and wondered what he could do to chase Doris away when she came tomorrow.

Chapter Three

"Good morning, Mr. Milne," Brooke Grundy said. Her cheerful tone matched her sunny smile and the light glinting off her blonde head as she stepped inside the house out of the nippy November air.

"How are you doing, Brooke?" Jess asked, unable to keep from smiling at the beautiful woman Blayne had married last year just a week before Christmas. At least that boy had the sense to know a good thing when he found it and not let it get away. In truth, Blayne and Brooke were so blissfully happy it did his old heart good to see the young couple deeply in love.

"I'm great, Mr. Milne. Are you feeling better?" she asked, giving him an inquisitive glance as she set a basket on the entry table.

Jess could smell cinnamon and wondered if it

came from Doris's applesauce muffins. Lest he show his interest in them, he focused on Brooke.

"I am feeling better every day, Brooke. And didn't I ask you to call me Jess instead of this Mr. Milne business?"

"Yes, sir," Brooke said, offering him a warm smile. "Grams said she'd be over at noon with your lunch and to check on you, but Blayne said to call him if you need anything before then."

"I appreciate that," Jess said, wondering if he'd choke on the bitterness clawing up his throat. Galled his daughter had left him at the mercy of Doris, there wasn't a lot he could do about it since he really did need the help, at least for a little while longer. Maybe he could call the doctor's office and see about hiring a home health nurse. That idea held much more appeal than putting up with Doris.

"I'm ready," Janet said, breezing into the room, rolling a suitcase in front of her.

"I'll take that out for you while you say goodbye," Brooke said, reaching for the suitcase. "Take care of yourself and have a good day, Mr..." Brooke grinned at him. "I mean, Jess."

"You be careful driving in that Portland traffic, Brooke. All of them are a bunch of idiots and crazies if you ask me."

"Yes, sir." Brooke smiled and took the suitcase outside, quietly shutting the front door behind her.

"Are you sure you have to leave, sweetheart?" Jess asked, wrapping Janet in a hug. "You could just stay here indefinitely and let those three unappreciative hooligans at home fend for themselves."

"I'm telling Steve he's been lumped in with the kids," Janet said, leaning back with a laugh. "You're going to do just fine, Dad. But I want you to promise you'll at least attempt to be nice to Doris."

Jess dropped his arms and shuffled back a step, grasping his walker when he nearly lost his balance. "I make no promises I can't keep."

"Dad..." Janet gave him a warning look. "I'll be checking in with Brooke and Blayne, so I better not get any reports about your bad behavior."

"Humph! More likely that wasp-tongued ol' biddy is the one who'll behave badly."

"Dad!" Janet admonished as she tugged on her coat and wrapped a scarf around her neck against the chill outside. She gave him another hug and kissed his cheek. "Please be good and take care of yourself, Daddy."

"I will, pumpkin. Now, you better get going. Brooke has better things to do than sit around waiting for you to start blubbering about leaving me."

Janet grinned, looking exactly like Julia as she cocked her head to one side and opened the door. "I promise no blubbering if you promise no yelling at Doris."

"Deal," he said, grabbing her hand and giving it one last squeeze. "Call me when you get home."

"I will, Dad. Love you."

"I love you, too, sweetheart." Jess stood in the open doorway and observed as she hurried down the walk and climbed in Brooke's SUV. She fastened her seatbelt then gave him a final wave. Tears burned the backs of his eyes as he watched the two women drive away, wondering when Janet had gotten so like her mother. Her smile, her laughter, even the way she walked reminded him of his wife.

Heartsore, he closed the door and started back to his chair. He detoured long enough to pull a stack of photo albums from a cabinet beneath a tall shelf of books by the fireplace and piled them on the coffee table. Rather than try to carry them all back to his chair, he sank down on the couch and picked up the first album.

Images of his wife as a brand-new, fresh-faced bride made him long for the days of his youth when his body was strong and obeyed his commands.

Julia had often told him she thought he was the most handsome boy in school. She'd even admitted she'd nearly fainted the first time he'd asked her on a date. He'd never seen a girl as pretty as her, or with such a tender heart.

His fingers trailed over her image as he recalled how nervous he'd been when he picked her up that first Friday night in his dad's 1959 Chevy Bel Air Coupe. Now that was a car to get the attention of girls. But the only girl Jess was interested in was sweet little Julia Phillips.

He'd taken her to the movies to see a comedy with Clark Gable and Doris Day. Somewhere between Julia drinking most of his Coca Cola and her laughing at the end of the movie, he'd fallen in love. That was March and they married in July. He remembered his folks and hers both telling them they were making a mistake, but they'd known the love they shared was the kind to last a lifetime.

Only Julia had left him alone long before he was ready to tell her goodbye. Honestly, he'd always figured he'd die first. If an accident on the ranch hadn't taken him, he assumed a health issue would, especially after Glen Grundy dropped dead of a heart attack out of the blue.

Yet, his perfect, amazing wife had died after a horrible bout with pneumonia had damaged her lungs and sent her into respiratory failure. Jess had remained by her bedside at the hospital for three days, begging her to fight, to live, to get well. She'd been incoherent most of the time, but she'd awakened once and told him she'd love him forever before she slipped away.

Jess sat back and felt moisture on his weathered cheeks. He hadn't even known tears had leaked out of his eyes. He fished a dark blue bandana out of his hip pocket, careful not to hurt his knee, and wiped his face then blew his nose.

He set the photo album on the coffee table and leaned his head against the back of the couch, closing his eyes.

"I wish it would have been me instead of you, Jules," he whispered before sleep overtook him.

"What do you think this is, Fort Knox? Last I knew, you don't have anything so precious in this house you have to keep every dang door locked."

The loud, irritated voice accompanying the slamming of the back door jolted Jess out of his slumber.

Startled, he sat up so abruptly he bumped his knee against the coffee table. He sucked in a gulp of acute pain and swallowed down a few words Janet would take him to task for saying.

More banging from the kitchen drew his gaze toward the doorway. While he'd slept, the formidable Doris Grundy had arrived.

"What's your problem?" he hollered and waited for the nausea that accompanied the pain to recede before he grabbed his walker and hauled himself to his feet.

He'd taken one step toward the kitchen when Doris appeared in the doorway, unwinding a dark red scarf from around her neck. She pulled a knit hat off her thick, wavy hair and fluffed it with her fingers before she unbuttoned her coat.

Jess did his best to ignore her rosy cheeks and the light sparkling in her gorgeous blue eyes. He'd always thought Doris had the prettiest blue eyes he'd ever seen. His Julia had soft brown eyes that always made him think of a graceful doe, but Doris's peepers were bright, intense, full of life and energy.

Quite like the woman currently glaring at him.

"I had to drag the bench by the back door over to where you have the spare key hidden in the rafters of the porch. Why have you got all the doors locked? Afraid someone will come in here and put you out of your misery?" Doris asked. She marched back into the kitchen before he could answer.

Apparently, she wasn't yet ready to put aside their differences and be on civil terms. Well, two could play that game. The promise he'd made to Janet to attempt to be nice to Doris crossed his mind, but he quickly dismissed it. The woman was more snappish than a testy turtle.

"Why didn't you just fly your broom up there and grab it?" he asked as he made his way into the kitchen. Although he kept his tone friendly, she spun around and snarled at him after tossing her outerwear on a chair at the table.

Jess barely suppressed a chuckle.

She took containers out of a basket and set them on the counter. "Are you hungry or not? I've got better things to do than mollycoddle a senile ol' donkey like you."

He moved his walker until he stood in front of her. Doris wasn't short by any means, but he stood several inches over her. He leaned down until his face was less than a foot from hers. "Senile ol' donkey, huh? You can do better than that." He bent a little closer. "What have those kids been doing to you over there on your place? It looks like you've gotten a dozen new wrinkles that are as deep as furrows. Aging you by the day, are they?"

Doris took a step back, flames shooting from her eyes.

Jess hadn't felt this good since before his surgery. He grinned and shuffled over to the table.

From years of spending time in each other's homes, Doris knew where to find the dishes and utensils. She spooned a serving of beef stew into a bowl, set it on a plate, added two pieces of still-warm cornbread and plunked it down in front of him.

He watched as she poured a glass of milk for him, a drink he still favored over all others. She set it on the table then moved back.

"You better eat while it's hot," she said, pointing to his plate.

He looked up at her as she reached for her coat. Surely, she wasn't going to toss food at him and leave. "Aren't you going to eat with me?"

"Are you sure you can stomach sitting across the table from an ancient hag such as myself?"

Jess offered her his most charming smile. "As long as I don't make direct eye contact, I'll somehow survive."

Doris muttered something he couldn't hear, but she dished stew in a bowl, took a piece of cornbread, and sat down across from him.

Jess waited until she'd placed a napkin on her lap to offer thanks for the meal, including a word of gratitude for the hands that prepared it. He might like to ruffle her feathers, but he was thankful Doris had brought him a meal and came to check on him. Janet had left several meals in the freezer, but he preferred Doris's plain home cooking to the fancy stuff his daughter liked to prepare.

"Did Blayne get that part he needed for the 4320?" Jess asked, aware Blayne had been trying to find a part for the old John Deere tractor. He dipped his spoon into the bowl of stew and took a bite. Doris might be a pain in his neck, but the woman sure could cook.

She gave him an odd look as she broke off a

piece of cornbread and drizzled honey over it. "He did find the part. I keep telling him he ought to give up on that tractor, but he refuses. When Blayne was little, Glen used to take him along all the time in that tractor and I think it holds good memories for him of his grandpa. Otherwise, he'd probably sell that thing and stop fussing with it. At least we have other tractors that are dependable to use."

Jess nodded, unwilling to share his similar reasons for keeping his old swather. Every time he'd thought about selling it, he'd remember the days when Janet would bring her blanket and doll and spend afternoons with him while he cut hay.

"It's a shame our kids had to grow up," Doris said, taking a bite of stew.

"It is." Jess filled his spoon, but glanced across the table at her. "If your grandson hadn't grown up, you wouldn't have a new granddaughter-in-law living in your house."

Doris smiled and her face softened. "I just love that girl like she was my own. Brooke might not have known a thing about country life before marrying Blayne, but she's picked it up quite well. She can cook, and she's never afraid to jump in to help wherever she's needed."

"Did she finally get over her fear of horses?" Jess asked, aware that Blayne's horses, particularly his team of Belgians, had scared Brooke half to death. "Seems to me a good ranch wife shouldn't be terrified of a horse as gentle as Spot. Shame about that girl being so scared of them."

Doris glowered at him. "She's learning to ride, although Girl and Boy still unsettle her a bit. What about your son-in-law? How many affairs has he had? Is it true he has six kids with four other women and one of them lives with him and Janet?"

Jess choked on the milk he'd been drinking and thumped the glass on the table. He pounded his chest a few times and coughed into the napkin Doris handed to him. The smug expression on her face didn't go unnoticed. He knew she was baiting him just like he'd tried to goad her with comments about Brooke.

"For your information, Steve has never done nor would he ever do anything of the sort. He teaches physical education and is the wrestling coach at the high school, a deacon at their church, and volunteers at the homeless shelter," Jess said when he could speak again. "Even if he had the inclination for an affair, which is so ridiculous I can't even imagine it, he's too busy for that sort of thing. Besides, he would never break his marriage vows. He's completely devoted to Janet and their kids and one of the most honorable men I know."

"Oh, I see," Doris said meekly, dabbing her mouth with her napkin while Jess took a vicious bite of his cornbread. She gave him a sympathetic look. "Steve's an overbearing brute. No wonder Janet views spending time as your nurse as a vacation. That poor girl. Has her husband always been horrid to her? Does he beat the kids?"

Jess felt cornbread crumbs go down the wrong pipe and again coughed into his napkin. His eyes watered, and he wondered if the sheriff would side with him if he throttled Doris. He took a drink of milk and straightened his shoulders. "Steve is a fine man, a great husband, and a very caring father. And you ought to know better than to suggest my headstrong daughter would put up with any nonsense when it comes to her or her children. I'm proud of both Steve and her."

"My mistake," Doris said with a dazzling smile that made it clear she'd intentionally tried to upset him.

He frowned at her. "As for my grandchildren, they are two of the nicest, most well-rounded teenagers you'll ever meet. Oh, but I forget, you don't have any young ones around to dote on, do you?"

Silence fell between them and Jess decided it was better than trading barbed insults about their offspring. He genuinely liked Brooke and thought Blayne was a lucky man, even if his wife was a little shy around horses. She made up for her lack of a rural background in many other ways.

And Jess knew Doris didn't mean a word of what she'd said about Steve or Janet. In fact, years ago when Janet first married Steve, Doris had mentioned to Julia how much she and Glen admired him and thought Janet had made a wise choice in a husband.

Had their relationship deteriorated to the point they couldn't even carry on a conversation without trying to inflict verbal harm?

Contemplative, Jess ate his stew and cornbread then watched as Doris slid two brownies onto a plate and set them in front of him. He ate them and drank the last of his milk while she did the dishes, stored the leftover stew in the fridge, and gathered her things.

"I'll be back with dinner at half past five. If you need something between now and then, call Blayne." She breezed outside, sweeping the tension that had filled the kitchen along with her.

"Well, that's that," Jess said, leaning back in his chair and drawing in a deep breath. He had no idea how he'd endure another day of Doris's presence in his home let alone a few weeks of her stopping in to check on him.

In the flurry of their anger at each other, he'd forgotten to give her the list of information Janet had left. It was probably better she didn't have it.

Jess shuffled to his recliner and settled in for a nap. Sleep had nearly claimed him when his phone rang. He grabbed it just before the answering machine picked up.

"Dad, I'm home and just wanted to let you know I made it with no problem," Janet said.

"That's great, sweetheart. I miss you already."

"I miss you, too, Daddy. Are you doing okay? Did Doris bring your lunch?"

"The cantankerous old sow did."

"Dad! You can't... you shouldn't..." Janet sighed. "Were you at least nice to her?"

Jess avoided answering by asking her how Steve and the kids were doing.

"Steve picked me up at the airport on his lunch break, but I won't see the kids until after school. Are you sure you're okay, Dad? Did you give Doris the information I left? Is she going to help with your exercises?"

"I forgot to give the info to her. I'm sure I can

manage the exercises on my own."

"We talked about this, Dad. You know you…"

Jess grabbed yesterday's newspaper and crinkled it near the phone. "I'm losing reception with you, sweetheart. I love you and I'm glad you got home safely. Bye, honey."

He disconnected and tossed the newspaper toward the garbage can, missing by several inches. Irritated with himself, with Doris, with his daughter, and life in general, he closed his eyes and went to sleep, wishing he'd wake up and find the last several years were just a bad dream and Julia would be in the kitchen fixing one of his favorite meals.

Chapter Four

"Grams, let me get that," Blayne said, taking the heavy box of food from Doris as she started out to her car with it.

"Thanks, sweetie," Doris said, hurrying ahead of him and opening the door to the backseat. He set the box on an old towel she'd placed down so nothing would spill on the upholstery.

"How did things go at lunch?" Blayne asked, opening her door and watching as she slid behind the wheel.

"As good as they can get with a nasty toad like Jess Milne."

"Maybe if you'd kiss him he'd turn into a prince," Blayne said, grinning at her.

"I ought to run over you for that comment," Doris said, starting the car. "Don't you have something better to do than pester the life out of me?"

"Actually, I do, but I wanted to make sure you knew Jess has some exercises he's supposed to do and he'll need help with them. Have fun." Blayne shut her door and backed away with a self-satisfied wave.

"Oh, he is so going to get his," Doris muttered, glaring daggers at her grandson as she swerved and pretended she planned to hit him.

Blayne slapped a gloved hand to his chest in mock dismay then laughed at her.

That boy was entirely too cocky for his own good. And he'd only gotten worse after he'd sweet-talked Brooke into becoming his bride. Blayne had spent the past year practically floating on cloud nine, clearly enjoying the honeymoon phase of his marriage.

She'd never heard him and Brooke fight, although they did like to argue their individual points. From what she could see, Brooke was as wild about Blayne as he was her. Brooke, who'd been abandoned by her father and lost her mother to cancer when she was a little girl, had never had a real home.

It pleased Doris to no end that Blayne's wife quickly considered the Rockin' G her home and fit in like she was always meant to be there.

Doris recalled what it had been like moving in with her mother-in-law as a young bride. It was a good thing she'd loved Glen to the point of distraction or she'd have left him after the first month of living under the same roof as his mother. That woman was impossible to please and thought her way was the only way to do anything.

To his credit, Glen always took Doris's side, but it hadn't really made things much easier or better. She was so glad when Glen updated an old cabin his grandfather had built when he'd first bought the place back in the late 1800s. They'd moved there after Doris had endured six months of listening to her mother-in-law berate her every move.

She recalled the woman chastising her for everything from the way she folded socks to how she kneaded bread dough. In spite of the fact the cabin was primitive, heated entirely with an old wood stove which she had to cook on, and they always had to battle mice and creepy-crawlies, she much preferred it to living in the big Victorian farmhouse with Glen's imperialistic mother.

They remained in the cabin even after their son was born, since Doris refused to allow her mother-in-law to take over raising her child.

They'd been married five years when Glen went to the house and found his mother dead in the kitchen. The doctor said her heart just gave out. Doris ruefully thought that was one thing his mother could have kept to herself instead of passing on the trait to Glen.

Glen's father asked them to move into the big house with him and they readily agreed. Their son grew up, went to college and then law school. He married a woman with dreams and ambitions equal to his own and opened a practice in Portland.

When Blayne was born, neither of them wanted to care for the boy. From the time he was three months old, he spent the entire week at the ranch. If his parents made an effort to work him into their schedule, he'd go to their condo in Portland on the weekends. However, all too frequently, he remained at the ranch. He hardly knew his parents and when they died, he mourned them more as a child would a distant relation than one who had just lost his mother and father.

For all intents and purposes, Doris and Glen had been the only parents Blayne had truly ever known. That was one reason why she loved him so much.

When Blayne had come home one day last year and announced his plans to marry the glass blower, Doris had gone into town the following afternoon and visited Brooke's shop. After seeing the way she interacted with people and doted on her adopted family of pot-bellied pigs, Doris realized Blayne had set his affections on a good, kind woman who was not only gorgeous, but smart and extremely talented.

Although he never asked for it, Doris silently gave him her blessing and supported him as he set out to win Brooke's heart.

Now, if the two of them would just get around to giving her a great-grandbaby, all would be right in her world. Well, it would be after she finished her unwanted duties of helping that detestable Jess Milne.

Doris pulled up at his house and parked on the side so she could go in the back door, assuming the idiot had most likely left the front one locked. She didn't know why everything he did and said infuriated her beyond the point of reason, but it did.

She got out of the car and had just opened the back door when one of the ranch hands hurried over from the barn.

"Can I help you with that, Mrs. Grundy?"

"Thank you so much, Pete. I appreciate it," she said, smiling at the young man then preceding him up the back-porch steps and inside the kitchen. She didn't bother to knock and Jess, who'd been getting a drink of water, almost dropped the glass when she barged inside.

"Look who's back," Jess said, offering her a rakish grin as he set the glass on the counter and turned to face her. "You blow in on a tornado? Have to hurry inside to keep a house from falling on top of you?"

Pete set down the box, his mouth dangling open in shock. He glanced from Jess to Doris and then slowly backed toward the door.

"I don't see ruby slippers on your clunky feet, you addlepated clodhopper, so I think I'm safe," Doris said. She dug a resealable bag from inside the box and handed it to Pete. "Thank you for carrying this for me. Enjoy the cookies."

"Yes, ma'am," the cowboy said. He made a quick escape, shutting the door behind him.

"It's not enough to traumatize me, but now you've added my crew to your list?" Jess asked, taking slow steps with his walker in the direction of the table.

Doris intercepted him halfway there, blocking his path. "I heard you have exercises you need to do, old man, and I mean to see they are done.

Where did Janet leave the list?"

Jess scowled but pointed to the end of the counter next to the old telephone mounted on the wall. "If you weren't as blind as a bat and equally as appealing, you might have noticed it there earlier."

Doris ignored his comment and picked up the note from Janet, thanking her for helping Jess, along with a detailed list of his medications, exercises, and doctor's appointments. It appeared he was due to see the physical therapist tomorrow as well as go in for a follow-up appointment with the doctor next week.

Barely restraining the urge to roll her eyes at the mess her well-meaning grandson had gotten her into, Doris studied the list of exercises then motioned for Jess to sit down at the table.

"I'd already be sitting if you hadn't gotten so goldurned high-handed with me," he said, easing into a chair with a grunt.

Doris slid a second chair closer to him then disappeared into the living room. She returned holding one of the throw pillows off the couch, dropped it on the seat of the chair, then gently lifted his foot onto the pillow.

She took an ice pack from the freezer, wrapped it in a dishtowel, pushed up the leg of the sweatpants he wore, and then placed the ice on his knee. "The note says to ice your knee for twenty minutes before and after you exercise. You do know you could do that without help, don't you?"

"I am aware of that fact," Jess said, adjusting the ice a bit then leaning back in the chair. "What makes you think I didn't already do the ice and exercises today?"

Haughtily, her nose inched upward in the air and she gave him a look full of disdain. "Janet mentioned she didn't have time to do them with you this morning and that you wouldn't do them unless under duress."

"Blabbermouth," he muttered, but loud enough she could hear.

Doris turned her back to him and emptied the box of food she'd brought for his dinner, setting a salad in the refrigerator and leaving the rest of the food on the counter. When he finished exercising, she'd warm up his dinner.

While he iced his knee, she checked to see if she needed to do a load of laundry and found Janet had washed the sheets from the guest room but hadn't had time to remake the bed. Doris did that then walked into the living room and straightened it, noticing the photo albums on the coffee table. She picked up the one that was open and grinned at the photo of Julia laughing at something Jess said.

She and Glen had always enjoyed a solid friendship with the couple. They'd been there for each other in good times and bad. Doris didn't know how she would have coped when Glen died if Jess and Julia hadn't stepped in and helped. Their steady presence sustained her through those first rough months until Blayne graduated from college and came home to stay.

Just as they'd been supportive and encouraging then, she'd done the same for Jess when Julia passed away. If they'd been good friends before, their shared grief and experience of losing a beloved spouse drew them even closer.

Then, one day, everything changed. Jess began to show an interest in her as a woman and Doris didn't like it. Not one bit. She'd made up her mind to never remarry because it felt like she would somehow betray Glen if she did. Not only that, but Julia had been a wonderful, sweet friend. To encourage Jess would have made her feel like she was cheating on her husband and her closest friend.

So she ignored Jess's attention, refused his invitations for dates, then finally made it glaringly clear she would never see him as more than a neighbor and friend.

The day of that conversation would be forever branded in her mind, since Jess had told her in no uncertain terms what he thought of her using Glen's memory as a shield for her cowardice. He accused her of refusing to reenter the land of the living since she preferred to cling to her grief and dwell in the past. He'd even dared to hint that she was afraid to love again because it hurt too much.

After she'd snapped back at him with a few comments she later regretted, he'd stormed off. They'd barely spoken for months.

Now she was stuck with him until he was back on his feet. Years of friendship had to be worth something, though, so she'd do this out of loyalty to their past closeness, to the fact Julia had been a dear, dear friend.

Doris turned the page in the photo album and studied an image of Jess. He had to be in his early twenties in the photo and looked like a movie star.

She'd always thought he bore a striking

resemblance to Harrison Ford. Jess had thick hair, broad shoulders, a handsome yet rugged face, and about the sexiest mouth she'd ever seen. He'd been a man that women noticed. It was good he'd always and ever had eyes only for Julia.

His wife used to laugh with Doris when women would try to flirt with him, fawning over him in town or at community events. When the first Star Wars movie came out in the 1970s, Jess and Julia had gone to Portland for a weekend getaway and he'd nearly been mobbed at a restaurant by women who mistook him for the actor. Julia had thought it was hilarious, but Jess had refused to go back to the city for more than a year.

Jess was still a good-looking man. His brown hair had turned silver, but it remained thick. His face bore wrinkles etched by sorrows and time, but his lips were still mighty tempting and his gray eyes piercing. For someone who was seventy-six, he had the physique of a man who kept in excellent shape, and his mind was as sharp as a tack.

If Doris was interested in getting married again, Jess Milne would have topped her list. But she had no interest or intention of going down that road. Not when she still missed Glen so fiercely and desperately, even ten years after his passing.

Glen hadn't been a looker like Jess, but he was the kindest, most noble man she'd ever known. She had no idea how he'd grown into such an honorable man with his horrible mother, but his father had always been good to her and to others. She assumed Glen took after the Grundy side of the family.

Doris was both pleased and relieved Blayne

was so much like his grandfather. Although she might be biased in her opinions where he was concerned, she knew Blayne was a generous, kind soul who offered strength and support wherever it was needed.

After all, his willingness to help others is what got her into this less than ideal situation with Jess.

Blayne had asked many times what had happened to make her so upset with their neighbor, but she refused to tell him. Part of the reason was because it wasn't any of his business. The other part, the part that kept her fuming at Jess, was what he'd said to her was the unvarnished truth and she didn't want to admit it or deal with it.

"If you're attempting to find hidden treasure in there, I don't have any. You'd do better to try and find the key to my safety deposit box," Jess hollered from the kitchen.

In spite of herself, Doris grinned. "I don't want your money or your treasures you dimwitted dolt." She carried the photo album back into the kitchen and set it on the table in front of Jess. "Julia was so beautiful. I used to envy how elegant she always looked."

"She was something special," Jess said in a soft voice, turning a page. His gaze lingered on a photo of Julia riding a horse and smiling over her shoulder at the camera.

Doris picked up Jess's foot and began his exercises. While she worked with him, she reminisced.

"Do you remember the time Blayne fell in that quagmire of mud in the northwest corner of the place when he was chasing a fox?" she asked.

Jess chuckled and nodded. They discussed things both Janet and Blayne had done that made them laugh.

Doris pretended not to notice when Jess winced in pain, but to his credit he didn't try to pull away from her or utter a word of complaint.

When she finished, a fine sheen of sweat covered his forehead and upper lip. She got a clean dishtowel and handed it to him, then settled a fresh ice pack on his knee while she got his dinner ready. After she served him a bowl of green salad with the vinaigrette dressing he liked and poured him a glass of milk, she heated up a plate of chicken and dumplings with spiced apple slices on the side.

Although she'd planned to go home and eat with Brooke and Blayne, Jess gave her such a pleading look, she warmed a plate of food and sat across from him while he ate and iced his knee.

Rather than continue insulting each other, Doris asked if he remembered the Thanksgiving Janet had dressed Blayne up like a turkey, complete with an assortment of chicken feathers glued to his shirt for a costume and made him sing a silly song with her.

By the time they finished eating the meal, Doris felt a bit of the kinship she used to feel toward Jess returning. She had no problem being friends with the man, if he'd leave it at that. Her concern rested in him wanting to take things further.

If he wanted a wife, she knew a dozen women in town who'd eagerly drag him down the aisle.

Doris grinned to herself as she did the dishes, wondering what those women would really do if

Jess said yes to one of them. Here they were in their seventies. Weren't they too old for thoughts of hugs and kisses and… She cut off her train of thought before it went any further off track and glanced over her shoulder at Jess.

"Do you need a ride into Romance for the therapist appointment tomorrow?"

"I can have one of the boys drive me in," Jess said, taking the ice off his knee and setting it on the table.

"I have to run into town for groceries anyway. It wouldn't be out of my way to take you." Doris could have easily asked Brooke to pick up the handful of items she needed, but she didn't want Jess to have to go to his appointment with one of the ranch hands. They were all busy with work as it was, and she had an idea he didn't like appearing weak or injured in front of them.

"Thanks, Doris. I appreciate the offer and I'll take you up on it." He gave her a long look then smirked. "You learn how to drive any better than you used to? The last time I rode in a vehicle with you, you nearly took out the Mackall's mailbox and drove up on the curb by Della's Diner."

Doris tossed a towel at him, catching him in the face. He laughed and dropped the towel on the table on top of the ice.

"If you'll recall, there were wasps in the car, coming out of the vents and you weren't paying any more attention to the road than I was." She stuck the ice pack back in the freezer, gathered the dishes she'd brought back into the box, then set a resealable bag full of cookies on the counter and a large piece of chocolate cake next to it. "If you want this cake, you'll have to get up and walk over here yourself."

Jess lumbered to his feet and used his walker to make his way over to the counter.

As he towered over her, Doris decided it might have been better if he'd remained seated at the table. He seemed far less threatening there than he did standing beside her as his warmth and presence seemed to envelope her.

Nervous, she shoved the cake and fork toward him and shifted to the other side of the counter.

"I better head home. Do you need anything before I go?" she asked, yanking on her coat and wrapping a scarf around her neck against the cold night air.

"You mean you aren't gonna stay and tuck me in and read me a bedtime story?" He batted his eyelashes at her and made such a goofy face, she couldn't help but laugh.

"No, you dunderhead. Behave yourself and I'll see you in the morning. We better plan to leave about eight-thirty since your appointment is at nine."

"I'll be ready."

Doris picked up her box and opened the door. Before she stepped outside, she felt Jess's hand on her arm.

She stood in the open doorway, frosty air swirling around them, and looked at him. A flicker of something in his eyes made her want to run out to her car, but she stiffened her spine and waited for him to speak.

"Thank you, Doris, for being a good friend."

"You're welcome. Now be a good boy and let me leave before you freeze. You might not be smart enough to stay out of the cold, but I am."

Jess spluttered something in protest, but she couldn't hear it as she slammed the door shut and marched out to her car with a broad smile on her face.

Chapter Five

Jess hummed as he took a shower, planning to be completely ready before Doris arrived to drive him into town.

He grinned, thinking of all the insults the two of them exchanged yesterday. At some point, he'd sensed a shift in her being hostile toward him to actually enjoying the banter. Perhaps all was not yet lost where she was concerned.

Irked he was in the position of needing her assistance, he would suffer through it. If their friendship returned to the easy footing it had always known, he'd gladly endure another knee replacement surgery although his other knee was perfectly fine. The one he'd had operated on had given him pain for almost twenty years. A horse he was riding stepped in a hole and went down on top of him, doing a number on his knee. Since then, the cold and rain had given him fits even if he refused to limp or let on that it bothered him.

The last time Janet was home she made him go to the doctor and accompanied him to make sure she didn't miss any pertinent details. She was surprised to hear the doctor say he'd recommended the knee replacement numerous occasions, but Jess never had time for it. Janet had made him schedule the surgery right then and there. She'd promised to come back when he had the surgery.

True to her word, she showed up two days before his surgery and helped him do a hundred little chores he wanted taken care of before he was down and out for weeks on end. While he was at the hospital, she baked and cleaned and put scads of single serving meals in the freezer.

Then three days after he came home, she announced she had to return to Salt Lake City and Doris Grundy would oversee his care.

Jess didn't know whether to be mad at Janet or send her a special gift of gratitude for leaving him at the mercy of his neighbor.

If the thawing trend continued with Doris's frosty behavior, he might just send his daughter a big bouquet of flowers. Shoot, he could even have Brooke mail her one of her fancy blown glass vases. While he was thinking about it, he made a mental note to ask Brooke for ideas for a Christmas gift for his daughter and granddaughter.

Jess let the steam of the shower relax his tense muscles, thinking of how much he'd enjoyed talking to Doris last night as they shared dinner. It reminded him of old times when they were nothing more than good friends. Perhaps the way to win Doris was from a place of friendship that could turn into something more.

He looked through the clear glass of the shower door to the shower chair he planned to haul out to the garage later. Although Janet had insisted he use the chair, he hated it. He'd set it out of the way when he stepped into the shower that morning. Anything that gave him a sense of being an invalid was on his list of things to get rid of as quickly as possible.

Today was the shower chair. Soon, he hoped to get rid of the elevated toilet seat that made him feel like a toddler being potty trained.

If his appointment with the doctor went well next week, he planned to ask for a cane instead of the blasted walker. The thing was too short for him, even though Janet had lengthened it as far as it would go. Evidently most people who used them were not a few inches over six-feet.

Jess squirted shampoo into the palm of his hand and rubbed it over his head. Eyes closed, he set the bottle back on the shelf but heard the soap plop onto the floor. He moved under the shower head to get the shampoo out of his hair, but his foot came down on the bar of soap. One moment he was upright, the next he was bouncing off the side of the tiled wall. He yelped as pain radiated from his knee and shampoo dripped into his eyes.

His next yelp was one of surprise when the bathroom door banged open and Doris Grundy raced inside.

Her eyes widened to the size of teacup saucers

when she realized he was in the shower. She took a step forward then froze, as though she couldn't decide if she should help him or leave. He grabbed the closest thing he could find and held it strategically in front of him.

"Are you okay? I heard you yell," she said, yanking off her gloves and stuffing them inside the pockets of her coat.

"I dropped the soap and hit my knee, but I'm fine." Jess blew suds of shampoo off his nose and blinked at the stinging sensation in his eyes. "What are you doing here so early? It's not even close to eight."

"Well, I brought over some breakfast for you and I thought you might need help with your shoes and… what not."

What not, indeed! Mortified at being caught in such a compromising situation, Doris made it worse when she cocked her head and grinned at him.

"I wouldn't have taken you for a pink piglet kind of fella, Jess."

He glanced down to see he held a ridiculous pink bath sponge with a smiling piglet face in front of him. "Mallory sent it as a joke when she heard about Pigtails, the little pig I brought home last month."

"Blayne mentioned you bought a pig to fatten up, but Janet said she didn't think you had it in you to eat it. If your little bath sponge is any indication, she's probably right."

"I'll have you know…" Jess lost his train of thought when Doris continued smiling at him with humor dancing in those magnificent sapphire eyes of hers. "Do you think I could finish my shower now?"

"Do you need the chair that Janet most likely put in there for you to use?" she asked, taking a step closer to the shower.

"No, I don't."

Doris gave him one more glance then turned her back to him. "Are you sure you're not hurt? I could have Blayne come help you."

"I don't need any help." He grabbed the bar of soap and hurriedly washed the shampoo from his hair and let the water soothe his burning eyes.

"I thought maybe when we go to town you might like to..." Doris's voice sounded strange and she didn't finish her thought. Jess glanced over to see her watching his every move in the mirror above the sink.

"You perverted old woman! Get out of my bathroom!" he hollered at her, but couldn't quite hide his grin.

Her cheeks bloomed with color, but she held his gaze in the mirror. "Thanks for the morning show. I'll have to tell the girls at book club all about this." Defiantly, she tossed her snowy white hair. "I now have answers to two of their most pressing questions. They'll be quite impressed."

"Out!" he bellowed and watched her move toward the doorway.

Heat seared up his neck and stained his cheeks with embarrassment, but he couldn't stop smiling. Doris left the bathroom, her giggles floating back to him. That woman. He would never have expected her to peep at him.

Then again, she was serving as his nursemaid of sorts. If the situation was reversed, Jess wouldn't have waited for permission to enter a room if he heard her scream in pain. He would have charged right in to see what was wrong and how he could fix it.

He wasn't sure if the pleased look on her face was from what she saw before he grabbed the piggy sponge or because of the idiotic pink sponge. Bless that Mallory for sending gag gifts to her ol' grandpa.

Doris scurried to the kitchen and opened the back door, fanning her overheated face. Mercy! She got more of an eyeful of her neighbor than she'd wanted. She knew Jess kept in shape from the hard work he did on the ranch, but she had no idea he looked so good beneath his western shirts. No wonder Julia had been so over-the-moon in love with him.

Chiding herself for thinking about such things at her age, she let the frosty air cool her searing cheeks.

She'd barely arrived and set a basket of food on the counter when she heard him yell in pain. She didn't think about where he was or what he was doing, she just reacted. Heart pounding, she'd raced on pure instinct into the master bedroom and flung open the bathroom door.

And there was Jess, in all his glory, looking as shocked to see her as she was to find him in the shower.

Then he'd whipped that little pink piggy sponge in front of him and Doris had to bite her cheek to keep from breaking into peals of laughter. The cute little snout and sweet smile of the pig taunted her as Jess held it in a strategic position.

She giggled as she closed the back door and removed her coat, hanging it on a hook next to Jess's outerwear.

Doris made coffee and gazed around the kitchen. From the first time she'd seen the house Jess had built for Julia, she'd loved the simple, open floor plan.

Not that she didn't like the historic house at the Rockin' G, but there were so many reminders there of her nasty mother-in-law. She'd often wished Glen hadn't been so set on investing money in restoring the old house instead of building something new.

Julia and Jess had lived in a tiny little two-bedroom house for years. When Janet was in high school and started having more friends over, Jess arrived home one day with a book of house plans and told Julia to pick out what she wanted.

Never one to put on airs or want more than she needed, Julia selected a very modest plan. Jess upgraded it, adding a spacious master suite and increasing the size of the living room and kitchen.

Now that they were getting older, Doris liked that the house was all one level. The stairs at her house kept her in shape, but there were times when she purely hated running up and down them all day.

But with Blayne, and now Brooke, there, they took care of more and more of the running. When Blayne got married, Doris moved from the upstairs bedroom she'd shared with Glen to a bedroom off the kitchen, wanting to give the newlyweds privacy.

She recalled how hard it was to be young and in love and have a mother-in-law hovering around all the time. At some point, she knew she should consider moving out of the house, but she couldn't bring herself to do it. Not yet.

Leaning against the marble counter, Doris sipped a cup of coffee and thought of the unexpected, interesting start of her day. A giggle escaped her, followed by another as the look on Jess's face floated through her mind.

"Oh, stop cackling like a witch," Jess said as he shuffled into the kitchen with his walker. Droplets of water clung to the ends of his thick hair, making it look darker.

He had on a navy blue shirt with stripes of gray that matched his stormy eyes. His cheeks looked smooth and taut from being freshly shaved, and the scent of his aftershave made her think of snowy winter pines.

He lifted one eyebrow in question and tipped his head toward the coffee pot. "You leave any of that bean juice for me?"

"I think I could round up a cup. I brought banana bread and a breakfast casserole. Think you can choke that down before we need to leave?" Doris asked, pouring a cup of coffee and setting it in front of him before she placed a plate in the microwave to warm his food. She buttered two slices of banana bread and slid them onto a bread plate. She set it in front of him, retrieved the plate with the casserole and gave it to him, then took a seat at the table.

"You already eat?" he asked.

"I had breakfast with the kids about an hour ago," she said, but bowed her head while Jess offered thanks for the meal.

"This is good," he said, biting into the banana bread. "You always were a good baker, Doris. Julia used to complain that she could never get her cakes as moist and light as yours."

"I had no idea," Doris said, surprised by his words. "Julia was always so good at everything she did. I don't think there's anything she couldn't do if she set her mind to it."

Jess chuckled. "She used to say the same thing about you."

Doris looked up at Jess and felt giggles beginning to build in her throat so she glanced out the window and watched Jess's ranch hands go about their morning chores. She saw one of the cowboys bend down and pick up a little pig. He said something to it before returning it to the warmth of the barn.

"Pigtails must have made a mad escape. Pete just carried her back in the barn," Doris said, motioning out the window.

At the mention of the pig, red crept up Jess's neck and stained his ears.

Doris hid a grin behind her coffee cup. She

could hardly wait until the next book club meeting to tell the girls what she'd seen. Then again, some things were better left unsaid.

Chapter Six

"How did you get lights up on your house, or did the boys do it?" Doris asked. She stood on the front walk and motioned to the strings of lights draped across the porch of the house.

Jess grinned as he stepped outside and closed the door behind him. Since Doris had started coming over to take care of him the previous week, she'd mentioned several times how sad his house looked without any decorations.

He'd asked the ranch hands to add a little holiday cheer to the place and they hadn't even grumbled too loudly about hanging the lights and setting up the outdoor decorations. They'd worked hard the previous afternoon to get it done in time to surprise Doris when she came today to take him to his doctor appointment. If all went well, he'd return home without his stitches.

"Magic," he said. "Don't you know Christmas is a time of wonder and anything is possible?"

"I think it's possible you're full of hot air and horsefeathers," Doris said, grinning at him. "I'll just go with the idea that you forced your overworked ranch hands to hang the lights on the house, barn, and along the fence. They sure do look nice, though, especially on this overcast, foggy day. If I didn't know better, I'd say it might snow."

Carefully, Jess made his way down the porch steps. "Now you're just being fanciful. It hardly ever snows here. I think it's just a typical winter day in Romance."

Doris's eyebrow shot upward. "Romance and blah skies seem far too contradictory. Let's call it a scene-setting mist, accented with frosty edges, as hearts turn toward the approaching holiday."

Jess shook his head and gave Doris a long look. "Ever thought of auditioning for one of the community plays? I think you'd do great at it with that kind of theatrical vision."

"Oh, hush up and get in the car, old man." Doris opened the passenger door to her car and waited as he eased inside then took his walker and set it on the backseat. After multiple trips in the car together, they'd established a routine.

Doris had no idea, and neither did the doctor, but he had plans and they didn't involve being an invalid for much longer. For now, Doris could think he needed her help so she'd keep coming over to feed him and harangue him to do his exercises. But he figured since he was already in better shape than most people his age and he'd been doing additional exercises to strengthen his knee, he ought to be back to normal in a few more weeks.

As soon as he could drive himself, Doris better watch out because he had every intention of going into courting mode. After the day she'd burst into the bathroom while he was in the shower, he'd seen interest lingering in her eyes. Sometimes he caught her watching him with a look that he could only interpret as longing.

Whether that stubborn, obstinate, infuriatingly wonderful woman wanted to admit it or not, she was as attracted to him as he was to her. This time around, he wasn't going to accept her half-hearted no as an answer. Not until she realized they both still had, he hoped, many good years of life ahead of them. There wasn't any reason for them to spend the time alone when they could enjoy the years they had left together.

Jess wasn't under any delusions where Doris was concerned. She was nothing like his soft-spoken, mild-tempered Julia. No, Doris was nothing like her. Opinionated, independent, sassy-mouthed and mule-headed, Doris was not the most peaceful woman he could pursue. But she was the one his heart wanted.

With Doris, he knew he'd never be bored. Never have a dull conversation. Never wish there was something to break up the humdrum routine of one day rolling into another. She was full of light and energy and life — exactly what he needed.

And if she'd just admit it, she needed him, too.

Regardless of his plans, he had to bide his time until the doctor cleared him to get back to a regular existence.

The trip into town took longer than normal with the fog making driving conditions hazardous, but Doris got them there with no problem. In spite of what he'd said about her ability to handle a car, she was a good driver. At least she was when wasps weren't swarming into the vehicle.

"Here we are," Doris announced as she pulled into a parking space at the doctor's office. She hopped out and handed him his walker while he got himself upright. Next time, he might suggest bringing Julia's old SUV or his pickup because they had to be easier to get in and out of than Doris's car. She kept step beside him and pulled open the door to the office then followed him inside.

Jess took a seat while Doris spoke to the receptionist. She'd barely settled into the chair beside him when Jess was called back.

"Want to come along?" he asked Doris, although he didn't know why. The words had popped out of his mouth before he could reel them back.

She shrugged and followed him and the nurse down the hallway to an examination room. In the small room, she took a seat on one of the plastic chairs while the nurse helped Jess onto the examination table.

The nurse took his blood pressure and pulse, recording the information in his chart, then left with a promise the doctor would see him soon.

"I hate these rooms," Doris said, looking around at the colorful posters on the wall and taped to the tiles of the ceiling.

"Why?" Jess asked. He had no fondness for them either, but Doris seemed wholly uncomfortable sitting on the edge of the ugly puce-colored chair.

"They seem so cold and sterile and impersonal, even with their attempts to make the room cheerful with the artwork." She pointed to a framed print of a butterfly landing on a bright pink flower.

"I guess I never gave it a lot of thought," he said, glancing up at the posters of hot air balloons taped to the ceiling. "It's not…"

"Hello!" the doctor said with a cheerful smile as he stepped into the room. He glanced at Doris and nodded in greeting before turning his attention to Jess. "Ready to get those stitches out?" he asked, pushing the leg of Jess's loose sweatpants up above his knee.

"I sure am and if you let me dump the walker, I'll be even happier." Jess forced himself not to wince as the doctor felt around his knee.

The man's non-verbal noises did nothing to reassure him until the doctor gave him a pleased look. "It's coming right along, even better than I hoped. Let's get those stitches out, shall we?"

The nurse assisted and in no time the stitches were removed. The nurse pulled the leg of Jess's sweatpants down to his ankle and stepped back. The doctor dictated while the nurse entered notes in Jess's file then he looked from Jess to Doris.

"You must be the one giving Jess such excellent care," the doctor said with a smile.

"I don't know about excellent care, but I've been making sure he's fed and does his exercises,"

Doris said.

"That's perfect." The doctor clasped his hands between his knees as he sat on a rolling stool and glanced over at Jess. "I'd like you to come back in ten days. We'll see how you're doing then. If you're healing as quickly as you've been the last two weeks, I might even give you permission to drive."

Jess grinned. "That's great news. And the walker?"

"Use it through the end of this week, then you can try the cane, but only if you have good balance. One fall and you'll be back to square one."

Jess nodded. "Anything else I need to know?"

The doctor glanced over some notes and recited a list of things Jess could expect in the following weeks. "The incision swelling and bruising should be completely gone by the end of the week. You should be back behind the wheel of your pickup between week five and seven. You may resume intimate…" he glanced at Doris then back at Jess, "activities in a few weeks."

Doris drew in such a startled gasp of air, Jess wondered if she'd suck the artwork right off the walls. The doctor raised both eyebrows and glanced at her then Jess.

Jess did his best to hide a grin and ended up covering his mouth with a fake cough.

The angry daggers shooting from Doris's expressive eyes might have sliced him to ribbons if he'd thought she really intended to inflict harm.

Her lips spread into a thin line. "I assure you, Doctor White, if there are activities of an intimate nature taking place, it most certainly is not with me!"

"I see," the doctor said, winking at Jess. "My apologies, ma'am. I didn't intend an insult but was just giving Jess our standard list of recovery expectations." He stood and placed a hand on Jess's shoulder. "Just don't overdo it, continue building your strength, and be back here in ten days."

"Hey, Doc, is it okay if I do things like attend a few community events?" Jess asked as the doctor opened the door to the room.

"Sure, as long as you are careful not to do anything that might hurt your knee. I wouldn't recommend standing on it, especially in the cold, for extended periods of time, but you'd be fine to attend the tree lighting or that sort of thing, if that's what you have in mind." The doctor gave Doris another look. "You folks have a good day."

The nurse helped Jess off the table and walked him out to the waiting room with Doris trailing behind, looking like she'd just drained the juice from a whole bucket full of sour lemons. The nurse handed her a cane for Jess to use later in the week.

For a moment, when he smirked at her, he thought Doris might just wallop him over the head with it.

Instead, she marched out the door, back ramrod straight, and headed for her car. She opened the door for him and tossed his walker in the back with his cane, but as soon as she was behind the wheel, she started the car, turned on the heater, then pinned him with a venomous glare.

"What did you say to the doctor to make him think that we're... that I would... that you and I..."

She looked as though she wanted to strangle him as her hands clenched the steering wheel until her knuckles turned white. "I'll have you know I'm not that kind of woman, Jess Milne. Don't you go spreading any rumors or getting any ideas about me that are not true and are never going to happen!"

"You were sitting right there in the exam room with me. Unless you'd jammed your ears full of cotton, you're well aware I never said anything to indicate you and I are... well, I didn't mention you," Jess said calmly. He admired the bright pink color of indignation painted across her cheeks. "I assume what he shared is just standard information he provides to everyone and didn't mean anything by it."

"Humph!" Doris gave him another long icy glare before she backed out of the parking space and drove through town.

Jess had hoped she'd be willing to have lunch with him, but he doubted he could talk her into stopping anywhere in her current mood. It was debatable if she'd even stop at his house instead of opening the door and giving him a shove when she passed by the ranch.

Amused by his ponderings, he glanced out the window to hide his smile from her. As they drove along the street, he spied something that might get Doris to stop.

"Oh, look at that. Brooke's decorating her window. Did she make those snowflakes?" Jess asked, turning to glance at Doris. "Do you think she'd help me pick out something to send to Janet and Mallory?"

Doris appeared to soften at the mention of his daughter and granddaughter. "I'm sure she'd be happy to. Would you like to go in?"

"If it isn't too much trouble," Jess said, sounding like a little boy who was begging for the teacher's approval.

Doris tossed him a wary frown but circled the block and parked in front of Blown Away, Brooke's glass blowing shop. Located across the street from the town's square, Jess studied the gazebo, already decorated with lights, garlands, and bright red bows, lending a festive air to the structure.

In fact, most of the businesses in town were decked for the holidays, and Brooke's shop was no exception. Garlands and lights rimmed her big display windows and an evergreen wreath hung on the door. Even though December was a few days away, it appeared the residents and businesses of Romance were more than ready to welcome the Christmas season.

"Come on, it's too cold to stand out here gawking," Doris said, setting the walker in front of him as he got out of her car.

Quietly, Jess followed Doris inside Brooke's shop.

"Hey, Grams! I didn't expect to see you today," Brooke said. She hurriedly hung another glass snowflake in the window then moved out of the display and greeted them with a broad smile. She gave Doris a huge hug, as though she hadn't seen her in months rather than that morning before she left the ranch. Brooke was as tall if not taller than most men Jess knew, and her height always caught him by surprise.

Jess smiled as Brooke gave him a gentle hug, acting afraid of somehow hurting him. "That Blayne is a lucky fella. I think you just get prettier every time I see you, Brooke."

The woman blushed but appeared pleased by his compliment. "How did your doctor appointment go, Jess?"

"Good. My stitches are gone, and I might even get rid of this walker soon."

"That's wonderful news." Brooke motioned to where a large coffee pot rested behind her front counter. "Would you like something hot to drink? I have coffee or I could make tea."

"Coffee would be great. I like it black," Jess said, looking around the shop, noticing Brooke had many Christmas pieces on display as well as a variety of other items like vases, bowls, and platters. He walked over to a tree made of twisted iron that had little hooks fashioned right into the ends of each branch and studied a clear ornament shaped like a teardrop with a beautiful snowflake inside the glass. The design almost looked frosty with its delicate, feathery lines.

"Blayne got one of his friends to make this display tree for me. I love it," Brooke said, handing Jess and Doris cups of coffee. He noticed Doris's appeared to have a generous helping of cream. If he remembered correctly, it would be sweetened with two scoops of sugar.

Jess took a sip of the good, strong coffee. "It's a clever way to display ornaments. Certainly draws your attention to them." He took another sip, watching Doris out of the corner of his eye. She stood beside Brooke, doing her best to ignore him as she looked around the shop.

"I don't know how you do what you do, Brooke, but I can see why people say you have a rare talent. The snowflake in that ornament looks like something from a fairy tale." He grinned at Brooke. "I don't suppose it's for sale."

She nodded. "It is for sale. In fact, anything you see here in the showroom is up for grabs." Brooke tipped her head toward Doris and winked at him.

Doris scowled at her then walked over to a built-in shelf that held an assortment of vases, pitchers, and glasses.

"Well, in that case..." Jess stared at Doris's back then looked at Brooke. "I'm shopping for gifts for my daughter and granddaughter. I think Mallory would love that ornament."

"I think she would, too," Brooke said, lifting the ornament off the tree and carrying it over to the counter. She pulled a small box from beneath the counter and carefully wrapped the ornament in bubble wrap, then tissue, before nestling it into more tissue inside the box. "What does Janet like?"

"Well, she has a lot of pine cone stuff she sets out during the holidays," Jess said, recalling the decorations he'd seen at his daughter's home when he'd been there last year.

"She might like this," Brooke said, showing him a bowl with pinecones and pine branches in the design of the glass. The bowl rested on three feet made of glass pinecones.

"She'd love that," Jess said, then pointed to a shelf nearby that held animal figurines. "How about that polar bear family. Mallory loves polar bears."

"Great choice." Brooke took the three polar bears and the bowl back to the register and boxed them while Jess continued to look around.

He made his way around the shop and stopped near Doris in front of the deep shelves full of colorful blown glass.

"What's that design? It looks like feathers," he asked, reaching out and touching a vase that made him think of peacocks, both with the design in the glass and the rich teal and blue colors.

"I call that peacock glass," Brooke said, stepping behind him. "In the light, it looks luminescent." She picked up the vase and held it up so the overhead lights reflected off it.

"Let's add that for Janet."

"Perfect," Brooke said, smiling at him while tilting her head toward Doris again. "You know, it's been pretty quiet this morning. I was thinking about taking an early lunch and indulging in some good Mexican food. I don't suppose you'd like to join me so I don't have to eat alone?"

"Oh, sweetheart, we wouldn't want you to eat alone," Doris said, placing her hand on Brooke's arm. "Of course we'll join you." She gave Jess a hard look, daring him to argue.

Meekly, he nodded. "I reckon that would be just fine."

"Great. I'll wrap up your purchases, Jess, then we can head over."

He made his way back to the counter and paid

for the gifts, then took a seat in one of the two chairs Brooke kept in a little area near the front of the showroom where impatient husbands tended to wait while their wives shopped.

It didn't take long for Brooke to wrap the gifts and return with them tucked into a large gift bag with her store name emblazoned across the front.

Jess stood and started to take the bag, but Brooke retained her hold on the handles. "I can carry it out to the car for you, and then we can grab lunch."

"I'll take that, sweetheart," Doris said, grasping the handles of the bag. "You get your coat and lock up while I put it in the trunk."

Brooke nodded and disappeared into the back, returning with her coat and purse. Jess stood on the walk in front of the store while Brooke locked the door and Doris slammed the lid on the trunk of her car.

He walked between the two women as they made their way past The Good Egg, a great place for breakfast, then waited for a few cars to pass before they crossed the street to El Torero. The scent of onions and seared meat filled the air as they stepped inside, making Jess's stomach growl with hunger.

Fortunately, the music playing in the background kept anyone from hearing it. Five minutes later, they were seated at a table, dipping warm tortilla chips into bowls of fresh salsa while they waited for their orders to arrive. Doris made sure she sat by Brooke in the booth. Jess sat across from them with his leg stretched out to one side.

"Everyone's excited about the tree lighting," Brooke said, breaking the silence that had fallen between them. "Will you be able to come into town for it, Jess?"

"I'd sure like to," he said, wondering how he could convince Doris to go with him.

"Why don't you ride with us?" Brooke asked. "Blayne is on the tree committee. This year's tree is a real beaut."

"Is it a noble fir? They are just an all-around great Christmas tree," Jess said, knowing Doris always choose a noble fir for the tree at her house, although Julia had always preferred a Douglas fir.

"It is a noble fir, and it's thirty-feet tall."

Jess whistled softly. "Now, that should be something to see. I wouldn't miss it. If you don't mind giving me a ride, I'd sure appreciate it."

"Great! We'll be by to pick you up about an hour before the fun begins. Blayne has some things he'll have to help with before the lighting."

"I'll be ready and waiting." Jess smiled at the young woman then gave Doris a glance. She hadn't stopped scowling at him since they'd sat down. He had no idea what to do to sweeten her disposition, but he'd give it some thought.

"Did you see the Esmerelda Theater has some wonderful Christmas shows planned?" Brooke asked, leaning back when the server brought their food.

Jess couldn't wait to slice off a bite of his carne asada. Accompanied with sides of rice and beans, it looked delicious. He couldn't remember the last time he'd been to the Mexican restaurant for a meal.

"Do you need anything else?" the server asked, looking around their table.

"This looks great, honey, thank you," Doris said, smiling at the young woman.

The girl nodded and left them to their meals.

"I haven't seen the movie list for the theater. When will they start?" Jess asked as he picked up his knife and fork.

"The week after the tree lighting. I think *Christmas in Connecticut* and *The Shop Around the Corner* are the first two scheduled to run." Brooke took a bite from her taco salad.

"Julia loved to watch *Christmas in Connecticut*," Jess said, feeling wistful. "I haven't seen that movie in years."

The way Brooke nudged Doris with her elbow didn't escape his notice, but he didn't mention it. Perhaps with Brooke in his corner, and Blayne encouraging his interest in Doris, they could help him in his efforts to win her over.

Jess asked Brooke about some of the other festivities planned during the holiday season which segued into a discussion about the various businesses in town.

By the time they finished lunch, Jess felt less out of touch with his community thanks to Brooke's knowledge of what was happening in town. With her shop in such a prime location, he supposed she probably saw a lot of what transpired in Romance.

Not only that, but Blayne was involved with numerous committees and groups. Between the three Grundy family members, there probably wasn't a lot that took place in Romance they didn't know about.

"Are you ready to head home, Jess? I'm sure it's past your nap time," Doris said, smiling sweetly although her eyes still flashed with indignation and anger.

Irritated by the way she made him sound like a cranky child in need of an afternoon rest, he returned her glare. He'd never admit how tired he was or that he longed for the comfort of his recliner, though. "Is there anywhere you want to go? I hate to be the reason you cut your trip into town short."

Doris narrowed her gaze, giving him a long, observant glance. "I have nothing else I need to do in town today. It's probably best if I take you home."

Brooke started to take the bill when the server brought it, but Jess snatched it from her with a grin. "My treat. It's not every day I have the pleasure of eating lunch with two beautiful women."

"You are full of flattery, aren't you?" Brooke said, smiling at him.

"Full of something, all right," Doris grumbled.

Jess swallowed down a chuckle as he took out his wallet and paid the bill. Brooke handed him his walker and the three of them made their way outside into the cold afternoon air.

Two women stood in front of Brooke's shop peering in the windows, so she hugged Doris, smiled at Jess again, then hustled across the street.

"Don't you miss the days when you had that kind of energy?" Jess asked as they watched Brooke's bouncing steps and the warm greeting she gave her customers.

"Who says I don't still have it?" Doris said, giving him a saucy grin as she snapped her fingers in the air and sashayed across the street. She glanced over her shoulder at him and his heart flipped in his chest.

Jess shook his head and followed along behind her, wondering what she'd do if he took her in his arms and kissed her right there on the corner.

The endless possibilities of how badly she'd react made him work to subdue a laugh as they made their way back to her car.

Chapter Seven

"Thanks for giving me a ride, Blayne. I sure appreciate it," Jess said, as he slid onto the passenger seat of Blayne's pickup.

Doris noticed it seemed far easier for him to get in it than to fold himself into her car. The next time she had to take him to town, she'd make sure to bring Blayne's pickup or drive Jess's.

The man looked over the front seat and smiled at her. "You look lovely as always, Doris."

His simple words of flattery made butterflies flutter in her stomach. If she'd been one of the twitterpated blue-haired ninnies who constantly tried to pry details about Jess Milne out of her, she might have batted her eyelashes at him or offered him a coy, encouraging glance.

Nonetheless, she was far too sensible and determined to remain aloof to his attentions to partake of such idiocy. Instead of acknowledging the warm feeling his presence gave her or how much his compliment pleased her, she frowned at him. "And you look like you'll freeze to death. Is that coat warm enough for you?"

From spending time with him the past few weeks, she knew anytime she asked him a question like that, one an adult might ask a clueless child, it made him so annoyed, he'd turn quiet, almost sulky. She needed for him to be irritated at her. That was better than allowing him to stoke the nearly overwhelming interest she already felt for him. He didn't usually pay her so many compliments, but he seemed intent on pouring on the charm this evening.

Blayne glared at her in the rearview mirror, but Jess merely continued to smile at her. "Why, thank you for asking, Doris, but this is a warm coat. Janet bought it for me a few years ago. It's got one of those fancy linings that can withstand cold temperatures to twenty below, so I think it should keep me plenty toasty for tonight. That's sure a pretty coat you're wearing. Is it new? It definitely sets off the beautiful color of your eyes."

Involuntarily, Doris's hand brushed along the front of her sapphire blue wool coat. It had been a gift from Blayne and Brooke for her birthday. She wore the matching hat, scarf and glove set that went with it. Brooke had told her the color was positively made for her to wear.

"It was a gift," she said, then looked out the window. She wished Jess would turn around and leave her alone. Had he figured out she treated him like a misbehaving boy just to frustrate him? If he had, she'd have to come up with a new method for keeping him an arm's-length away.

The reason why she had to work so hard to do that was one she didn't want to contemplate or examine. The less time she spent thinking about Jess, about how much he meant to her, how deeply she valued his friendship, the better.

Since she'd been helping him after his surgery, she'd recalled all the reasons they'd been friends. Jess had a great sense of humor and could make her laugh like no one else. They shared the same morals and values, even if the rascal liked to tease her right up to the edge of her tolerance far too often. In spite of how much he could irritate the dickens out of her, he was intelligent and easy to talk to. He'd given her good advice about everything from some investments she'd made to his thoughts on a gift she wanted to get Blayne for Christmas.

When she wasn't pretending to be mad at him, Jess was about the best friend she'd ever had. She just didn't understand why the man couldn't leave well enough alone. Although he hadn't asked her out on a date, he continued to hint he'd like to be more than friends.

Surely he knew how utterly preposterous it was for them to consider a romance at their ages. It wouldn't be long before they were heading for a care home. Then again, they'd never been typical senior citizens. Jess could have easily passed for a man fifteen years younger. Doris liked to think she looked younger than her age, too.

The last time she'd gone to Portland with Brooke, a man who couldn't have been more than fifty-five shamelessly flirted with her until he found out she was in her mid-seventies. Even then, he didn't seem entirely deterred by her age. Brooke had teased her about it the whole way home.

That man's profuse words of adoration hadn't meant a thing to her. And they certainly didn't make her limbs feel weak and languid. Not the way a single look or a few genuine words of kindness from Jess could make her feel.

"Isn't that right, Grams?" Blayne asked, looking at her in the rearview mirror again.

"I'm sorry, sweetie. I didn't hear what you said." Doris leaned forward and placed her hand on Blayne's shoulder. "What did you ask?"

Her grandson gave her a knowing look, as though he could sense her thoughts about Jess. Blayne smirked at her in that infuriating way he had that made her long to smack him.

"I just said the plan is for us to attend the tree lighting and grab a bite to eat before we head home. Right?"

"Yes, that's what we talked about at breakfast. I'm sorry Brooke is unable to get away from the shop until right before the tree lighting," Doris said. With Brooke along, there would have been an additional buffer to draw Jess's attention away from her.

He and Brooke seemed to get along famously. For that matter, Jess and Blayne had always gotten along well, too. After Glen died, Jess had become more like a beloved uncle to Blayne than just a neighbor. She knew Blayne had often turned to Jess for advice when it was something he didn't feel comfortable discussing with her.

Whether she wanted to acknowledge it or not, their families had been not just merely connected but intertwined for years and years. Before she could give further thought to what that meant, Blayne drove into Romance and headed for the town square where it appeared people were already congregating. Some of the civic groups had set up booths selling hot chocolate, cider, and German sausages.

He drove his pickup right up on the sidewalk and stopped.

"You can't park here," Doris said, embarrassed when everyone looked their way.

"I know that, Grams, but once you and Jess get out, I'll go park behind Brooke's shop. I don't want Jess to have to walk any further than necessary."

"I appreciate that, Blayne," Jess said, opening the door and sliding out. While Doris was still gathering her gloves and scarf, Jess opened her door and held out a hand to her.

Hesitantly, she took it and allowed him to help her to the ground. He immediately released her fingers then reached into the back of the pickup and took out his walker.

"Shall we go stake out a good place to watch?" Jess asked, closing the door and giving Blayne a quick wave as he backed up and drove down the street.

"Yes, let's do that, then I'm going to get a cup of hot chocolate."

Ten minutes later, Jess sat on the seat of his walker, sipping hot cider while she stood beside him with a cup of hot chocolate. Together, they watched Blayne and the other committee members rush around, making final preparations.

Doris jumped and nearly spilled her drink when a hand settled on her shoulder. She glanced up at Brooke's smiling face.

"Hey, Grams."

Doris hugged the woman she loved like her own daughter or granddaughter. "You startled me, honey. I'm glad you could finish up and come over before things got underway."

"Oh, I wouldn't miss this, even if that hunky husband of mine wasn't right in the middle of it all." Brooke grinned and pointed to where Blayne worked with two other committee members. She turned to Jess and placed a hand on his arm. "How are you? Can I get you anything?"

"I'm doing great, Brooke, but thank you for that offer," Jess said. "Blayne mentioned getting dinner after this is over, but those sausages sure smell good."

"I don't think Blayne will care if we eat here or somewhere else. I can get you both sausages to eat now if you want," Brooke offered.

"Let's wait a bit," Doris said, glancing to Jess for agreement. He nodded and went back to sipping his hot cider.

"Is Chase performing tonight?" Jess asked as Blayne spoke with music star Chase Lockhart. The singer happened to be engaged to Izzy Sutton, a woman who ran a bed and breakfast in Romance.

"You'll have to wait and see," Brooke said with a teasing smile. "I'm going to go get something hot to drink. Are you sure you two don't want anything?"

"How about some of those doughnuts the bakery booth has over there?" Jess motioned to a busy booth.

"Done," Brooke said. She refused the twenty-dollar bill Jess tried to give her and hurried across the square to the vendor booths.

"She's sure a nice gal, Doris. Blayne couldn't have chosen any better." Jess glanced over at her. "You seem to be fond of her."

"I am fond of her. I love that girl like she's always been a part of our family. Brooke and her little pigs fit right in with us."

Jess grinned and turned toward her. "How are the pigs? I haven't heard anyone mention chasing down Tigger for a while."

"They're doing great. Winnie is as sweet as ever and Roo is about the most adorable little thing. She loves to cuddle and if you sing the theme song from *Winnie the Pooh*, she'll grunt along with it like she's singing, too." Doris raised an eyebrow and leaned toward him conspiratorially. "She might be my favorite little piggy, but don't tell the others."

"Your secret is safe with me. But what about Tigger?"

"After Blayne triple-reinforced the fence in his pen last month, he's only managed to escape twice, and both times were when one of the hands forgot to not just latch the gate but lock it."

"And here I thought Tigger was coming over

and teaching Pigtails a few of his tricks."

Doris smiled. "I could bring him over if you want. I'm sure he has some escape maneuvers Pigtails has not yet mastered."

Jess chuckled and shook his head. "Don't you go getting any ideas. My slab of bacon on the hoof doesn't need any help finding trouble."

Doris playfully whacked his arm with her gloved hand. "You, and everyone else, know Pigtails is not going to end up as bacon. Janet said you're turning into a real softie in your old age."

He shrugged. "Maybe I am. What of it?"

"Well, maybe it's not a bad thing at all, Jess Milne."

He turned his arresting, smoky gray eyes on her. She could see interest, curiosity, and hope mingling in their depths. Even in his current state of healing from a surgery, Doris thought Jess was a handsome, striking man.

Tonight, he wore a black cowboy hat with his dark gray coat. His jeans were creased down the front of the legs and he wore a pair of thick-soled work cowboy boots. When he smiled at her, her traitorous heart began pounding and she felt like her breath had been sucked right out of her.

Daphne, at the book club, was right. Doris needed to stop reading so many romance novels. They were starting to get to her. At least that was the excuse she used for the fact she couldn't stop looking at Jess.

"Blithering ninnies," she muttered to herself. That's what her book club members were turning into. A bunch of blithering, harebrained, love-starved ninnies.

"What was that, Doris?" Jess asked innocently, although she had a good idea he'd heard her.

She was saved from responding by Brooke's return with a bag full of eggnog doughnuts and a cup of hot cider.

"Mmm. This cider hits the spot, but it's not as good as yours, Grams," Brooke said, standing beside her.

Doris wrapped an arm around Brooke's waist and gave it a squeeze before she helped herself to a doughnut. The texture and taste were different, but delicious.

"I might have to see if I can pry this recipe out of them later," Doris said, taking another bite of the doughnut.

"If you need someone to taste-test for you, I'll volunteer," Jess said, finishing his doughnut and wiping his fingers on a napkin Brooke took from her pocket. He nodded to her in thanks before his attention focused on Doris again.

She wanted to squirm under his perusal but forced herself to hold still and watch Blayne and the others scurrying around.

"Doris said you picked out this coat for her, Brooke. I don't think you could have found one that matched her beautiful eyes any better and that hat really sets off her white hair." Jess gave her a cocky grin. "Maybe she should audition for Mrs. Claus this year."

Doris scowled at him. She knew she was old and white-headed, but she wasn't chubby like Mrs. Claus. Was he inferring something about her size?

Or was she just prickly because of her own tumultuous feelings about the man?

Rather than respond, she excused herself and walked through the gathering crowd. She waved at Lucas Chase and his wife, Dori. Lucas owned the local heating and plumbing business. After Dori started helping with it, business had really picked up for him.

She watched several newly married or recently engaged couples. It seemed Romance had certainly been living up to its name in the last year.

Doris turned around and nearly bumped into the protruding belly of Katie Mackall Elders. The young woman grinned as she held onto her husband's arm.

"Katie, honey, how are you?" Doris asked giving the girl a hug then smiling at Mike Elders. The couple had wed close to the same time as Blayne and Brooke last December. Only Katie and Mike hadn't wasted any time in starting a family. "Are you counting down the days until this little bundle of joy is here?" Doris gently touched the mound beneath Katie's coat.

"I can't believe we'll be parents soon," Katie said, smiling up at Mike in adoration.

"Well, I'm ready for that baby to arrive. The rocking chair is polished and ready to put to good use," Katie's Aunt Viv said as she and her husband, Earl, approached.

Doris spoke with them a few moments, then gave Katie another hug. "If you ever need a babysitter, give me a call," she said, then left them as she continued wandering around the square.

She watched Savannah Miller speak to a young man she thought was the Potter's grandson, Baxter. Doris didn't know he was back in town. From the looks on the faces of the two young people, they didn't appear pleased to run into one another.

"Hmm. Interesting," she whispered to herself, then continued scanning the crowd. She waved to Brent and Nicole Todd and Nicole's son, Tony. Brent owned Finding Forever Animal Rescue where Brooke had gotten her beloved pigs. Sometimes Blayne took animals Brent didn't have room for, especially the larger ones.

Most of the time Brent found homes for them, but a few had stayed. That was how the Rockin' G came to be home to Donkey Kong, a sweet little donkey that was only supposed to be at their place for a week or two but found a permanent home with them. Doris had kept dozens of chickens over the years, and they'd even had an alpaca come through in the summer. Brooke would have kept it, but Blayne assured her it would be better off at the home Brent found for it with other alpacas.

Doris spoke to Mary McKay, a woman she'd known for decades who was in charge of the annual *A Christmas Carol* production. Some of Mary's grandchildren were in the play, and Doris was among the members of the Romance Christian Church Choir who would perform during the production.

After bidding Mary a pleasant evening, Doris made her way over to where Brooke spoke with Jess. The man said something that made Brooke laugh and Doris couldn't help but smile. Jess might be a royal pain, but he was a good man.

Doris joined them at the same time Blayne stepped behind Brooke and wrapped his arms around her. He pulled her back against him and kissed her cheek.

"I smell cider and doughnuts. Did you save any for me?" Blayne asked, nuzzling his nose against Brooke's neck.

She held up her half-empty cup of cider and Blayne took a long drink. Doris handed him a doughnut and then they watched as the mayor moved in front of the microphone and made several announcements.

Chase Lockhart took the stage and performed for a while. When he finished, they all waited for the big moment of the tree lighting.

"I sure hope this works," Blayne muttered a moment before the lights on the towering fir twinkled to life and everyone cheered.

Doris clapped then patted Blayne on the back. "Good job, sweetie! The tree looks great."

"It does look nice," Blayne said, "but we had plenty of good help." He kissed Brooke's cheek again.

"I like the white lights and red ribbons," Doris said, as she watched a few children race up and hang ornaments on the bottom branches of the tree. "Very festive."

"Anyone who wants can hang an ornament on the tree. Brooke and I are going to add one on our anniversary." Blayne gave his wife a look filled with love then glanced back at Doris. "Did you bring one to hang on it, Grams?"

"No. I haven't decided what I want to put on the tree. I'll hang one later, too."

"How about you, Jess. Do you plan to place an ornament on the tree?" Brooke asked.

"I hadn't given it a thought. Julia used to fuss about doing that and always found a perfect ornament to hang on it. I've entirely forgotten about the tradition." Jess grew quiet and Doris wondered if he was thinking about his wife. Out of the bonds of grief that united them, she sidled closer to him and patted his hand as it rested on his walker in a gesture of understanding and sympathy.

He turned his hand over and gently squeezed hers. An unreadable look on his face and eyes made her want to give him a hug, but she refrained. That might give the man entirely the wrong idea and she'd be back to calling him horrible names to keep him at bay.

"How about sausages and some of those curly fries for dinner?" Blayne asked. "We can eat them and watch the crowd."

"Sounds good to me," Jess said, giving Doris another long look before turning toward Blayne. "But only if you let me buy. You all have done so much for me the past few weeks, it's the least I can do."

Blayne looked like he wanted to refuse, but he finally nodded in agreement and took the money Jess held out to him.

"Come on, glass girl, you can help me carry everything," Blayne said, pulling Brooke along with him.

"They sure make a handsome couple, Doris.

When they get around to having kids, you might have to remodel the house, though. They'll be as long legged as giraffes."

Doris nodded in agreement. "Blayne's always been tall, and with Brooke at nearly six-feet I would be astonished if they have a short child."

"You started picking out baby names or planning how to decorate a nursery yet?" Jess asked in a teasing tone.

"No. I'll at least wait until they announce they're expecting. If Santa Claus got my letter, that's tops on my Christmas list."

Jess chuckled. "But you missed the part about being a very good girl to get on Santa's nice list."

Doris glared at him and fisted her hands on her hips. "If taking care of a flat-footed old fuddy like you doesn't earn me a permanent spot on that list, then nothing will."

Jess leaned over and kissed her cheek, much to Doris's shocked surprise. "And here I thought you were doing it out of the goodness of your heart. Now I find out there are ulterior motives of trying to bribe Santa. Shame on you, Doris Grundy."

Doris couldn't breathe let alone think. Jess leaned so close to her she could smell his shaving lotion blending with the intoxicating scent of him, which was warm, appealing, man. While most men she encountered their age smelled like arthritis cream or menthol, Jess always put her in mind of a western cologne advertisement.

"Oh, no," he whispered and stiffened.

Doris looked up to see half a dozen women from her book club hustling toward them. They looked like a pack of wild dogs about to descend on a fresh slab of prime beef.

Unaware of moving, Doris placed herself in front of Jess, protecting him from the advancing onslaught of wily widows.

"Doris! How delightful to see you this evening! And you too, Mr. Milne," purred Rosalind. That woman had convinced herself she was the object of every man's desire fifty years ago and still held the same opinion, despite the fact time had marched onward even if she hadn't. She dressed in outfits that had been out of style for decades, wore her hair in a style popular when Nixon was in office, and used what must have been a putty knife to apply thick sky blue eye shadow behind her mascara-clumped eyelashes. In spite of her fashion faux pas and sometimes questionable behavior, everyone put up with the woman. Rosalind's rich husband had left her a substantial life insurance policy to go along with his fortune when he died. She poured a good amount of it into various charities and enterprises in Romance.

The women literally pushed Doris out of the way to reach Jess. Starved for male attention, they encircled him in a cloud of stout perfume.

"Is Doris taking good care of you, Mr. Milne?"

"Do you need any help? I can give you a good back scrub in the bath."

"I'd be happy to move in and take care of you until you're back on your feet."

The women batted their eyelashes and fawned over him.

"If you need a little distraction from the pain,

give me a call," Rosalind said, slipping a card with her number into his coat pocket then brushing against his chest.

"Ladies, how nice of you to stop by and say hello," Blayne said, breaking into their midst. He carried a box of food while Brooke held another with drinks. "I hope you'll excuse us while we eat. Food is best enjoyed hot, you know." Blayne offered the women a charming smile before he moved to stand protectively in front of Jess.

"Of course, Blayne, darling. We were just catching up with a dear old friend," Daphne said, winking at Jess.

Doris wanted to snatch off the woman's Coke bottle-thick glasses and punch her in the eye.

"Rein it in Grams," Blayne whispered as he bent near her. He motioned to a table that had not yet been claimed. "Let's go sit there."

He and Brooke hurried over to set the food down and save the table while Doris followed with Jess.

"Those friends of yours are like..." Jess paused, as though he couldn't quite come up with an accurate description.

"Oh, just ignore them." Doris certainly planned to. The reason they'd all made her mad and irrationally jealous never entered her mind as she and Jess sat down across from Blayne and Brooke at the table and ate their dinner.

The air grew colder and Doris found herself scooting closer to Jess. Without thinking about what they were doing, he slipped his arm around her shoulders. He pulled her against his side, sharing the heat radiating off his big body.

Doris had the fleeting thought that it felt like she'd come home, but quickly pushed it away. Glen had been her everything — her husband, her friend, her confidante, her champion, her partner, her great love. It wasn't fair to let anyone else into her heart when she'd promised he'd have hers until death parted them. Even if death had claimed him, she felt it only right to honor her vows until her death, too.

But just for one evening, for an hour or two, she didn't want to think about her determination to never love again. For now, for this decadent moment, she just wanted to rest in the friendship and warmth Jess so willingly offered.

Blayne glanced at her once and smiled, then slipped his arm around Brooke, pulling her into the circle of his arms.

They remained that way until the crowd tired of visiting and began to disperse.

Blayne stood and looked down at Doris as he took Brooke's hand in his.

"Grams, do you mind driving Jess home? Since Brooke has her SUV here, I don't want her to have to drive home alone."

"Well, I…" Doris studied her grandson and his wife, aware of the loving looks they exchanged. "Sure, honey. I'll drive the SUV because I hate trying to reach the pedals in your pickup."

"Deal. I'll go get the SUV and drive it up to the curb," Blayne said, jogging across the street.

Brooke walked on one side of Jess while Doris flanked the other, both of them keeping an eye out for the pack of man-hungry widows. Thankfully, they seemed enthralled with a group from the senior center who'd arrived and were sitting on the other side of the square.

"The coast is clear," Doris said quietly, making Brooke and Jess both laugh.

Blayne pulled the SUV up next to a row of cars parked along the street and jumped out. He helped Jess inside, set his walker in the back, then kissed Doris's cheek.

"Don't get home past your bedtime, Grams."

She reached up and pinched his cheek. "Oh, go on with you!"

Blayne laughed and walked over to Brooke, placing his hand possessively at the small of her back as they meandered into the midst of the festivities.

"They really are good kids," Jess said as Doris moved up the seat and adjusted the height of it before she carefully pulled into the traffic.

"They are good kids." She turned onto a side street to avoid the line of cars on Main Street and drove through a few residential areas. Many homes already had lights up, twinkling in a rainbow of colors against the dark night sky.

Jess sighed. "I haven't driven around and looked at lights for years. Do you think that house over on…"

Doris turned down a side street before he could finish his statement. They drove past a stately home where lights dripped off the eaves and covered all the bushes and trees.

"It's as amazing as I remember," Jess said, staring out the window as Doris stopped in the street. No traffic was coming either direction, so they remained there a few moments pointing out the various lawn ornaments that had been added in recent years.

Jess laughed when she drove a few streets over and stopped in front of a home known for its wacky themed decorations. One year, they'd decorated their yard with a red-nosed reindeer and abominable snowman. Another year, they had Bigfoot terrorizing a herd of reindeer.

This year, it appeared they were going with a Grinch theme. The lawn looked like it had been vandalized, with ornaments tossed on their sides and hanging upside down. In the back, by the house, with a spotlight shining on him, was an illuminated life-size Grinch figure, holding two extension cords, as though he was about to unplug them.

"Where do they come up with this stuff?" he asked, still grinning as they drove away.

"I don't know, but it's always fun to see."

Doris headed out of town toward home. Even though it was cold, the roads were clear and it didn't take long until she was pulling up by the back door at Jess's place.

"Thanks for driving me home," Jess said, opening his door, but not sliding out.

Much to Doris's surprise, he reached across the seat and cupped her cheek with his big, rough hand. That touch, so unexpected, so comforting yet invigorating, left her thoroughly discombobulated and wanting more. It had been so long since anyone had touched her like that and she craved it. Craved the love and closeness she'd enjoyed so many years with Glen.

Jess pulled his hand back, gave her a rakish grin, then stepped out and retrieved his walker from the back seat.

"Thanks again for the ride," he said, then closed the back door of the SUV and made his way up the porch steps.

Doris waited to leave until she saw him flick on the kitchen lights and wave out the window.

Despite her determination to keep Jess from infiltrating the walls she'd built around her heart, he was perilously close to plowing right through them.

And that was something she couldn't allow to happen, no matter how much she wanted him to turn those walls to dust.

Chapter Eight

Jess leaned on his cane as he reached down and scratched Pigtails along her back. The little piglet grunted and twisted, clearly wanting him to get to a spot he hadn't yet reached. Unable to hunker down and give her the attention she obviously craved, Jess made his way to where a small bale of hay sat in the barn aisle.

"Jump up here, baby," Jess said, patting the top of the bale.

Pigtails squealed and turned in a circle three times before rubbing against his leg and grunting again, little curly tail switching back and forth like the rod on a metronome.

"Come on, Pigtails. Jump right on up here." Jess patted the hay again.

One of the ranch dogs ran in the barn and leaped on the bale, squirming and slobbering as Jess lavished it with pets and belly scratches.

Pigtails, clearly jealous of the attention Rooster received, squealed again then launched her little body at the bale.

Jess reached down and gave her a boost. The dog licked her face then hopped down and raced back out of the barn when one of the ranch hands called for him.

Pigtails wiggled her bottom, tail bouncing, as Jess pet her. "You're just a sweet lil' gal, aren't you, Pigtails. Yes, you are. A sweet lil' baby. Are you my best girl? Oh, I think you are."

"Well, that's just a shame to hear," a familiar voice said from the doorway, startling him.

He turned and watched Blayne Grundy walk toward him. Jess recalled years ago when Blayne's voice had changed. Seemingly overnight, he'd gone from a squeaky adolescent to having a deep gravel-laced voice that sounded like it belonged on a sixty-year-old man who'd spent his life chain-smoking. He knew that voice had driven more than a few girls to distraction during Blayne's teen years.

Although Doris probably didn't know it, Blayne hadn't been the angelic child she'd always thought him to be. He'd gotten into a little trouble in high school, pulling pranks and doing stupid things a group of sixteen-year-old boys tended to do when they got together and had a few illegal drinks.

One night, Jess and Julia had just gone to sleep when the phone rang. Blayne was calling from the police station. He'd been picked up in a car full of boys who'd been drinking and racing a pickup full of hooligans from a neighboring town.

Blayne had begged Jess to come get him and not tell his grandparents. Since the boy hadn't done anything like it before, Jess went and got him then burned his ears all the way back to the ranch. Rather than drive him all the way home, he made him walk from the road up the long driveway of the Rockin' G. He figured the hike gave Blayne time to think about what he'd done as well as the promise he wrangled out of the boy to never again be that stupid.

True to his word, Blayne had shaped right up. Jess had never told Doris or Glen he'd been the one to keep their grandson from spending the night in jail. Something about that night had established a link between Jess and Blayne that had only deepened over the years. Jess thought of Blayne as a grandson, not just a neighbor.

"What are you doing over here? Don't you have enough work at home to keep you from harassing me?" he asked the man.

Blayne chuckled and picked up Pigtails, giving her a good scratching on her back and belly before setting her on the hay bale. He crossed his arms over his broad chest and leaned against a stall door.

"The fact you consider the pig your best girl might just be why Grams is at home in a cranky mood. Don't tell me you've given up on her already? Or should I say again?"

Jess glared at him and walked into the stall where they kept Pigtails. The piglet followed him. He dropped a carrot into her food bowl then walked out while she was busy with the treat and shut the door, firmly latching it.

"Come on up to the house and have a cup of coffee," Jess said, limping past Blayne. Together, they made their way up the back-porch steps and into the kitchen.

They both hung up their coats and washed their hands. Jess took down two mugs then Blayne filled them both with coffee and carried them to the table. When they both were seated, Jess took a sip of the coffee and looked at the young man. "What do you suggest I do? I can't exactly sweep your grandmother off her feet."

"I know that, but Grams seemed about as happy as I've seen her in a long time when she thought you needed her help. Now that you're walking with the cane and can drive yourself again, she's been as out of sorts as a sore-footed pack mule at the end of a trail ride."

"That's cranky," Jess said, grinning at Blayne. "I'd be more than happy to have her come over every day and bring food, like she was before. I purely hate eating my own cooking, I don't care for the stuff Janet left, and I can't exactly show up at your place three times a day at meal-time. Doris has made it abundantly clear she's not interested in being anything but friends. I can't force her to care about me."

"You can't," Blayne agreed, "but you don't need to. Whether Grams admits it or not, she likes you, and I mean much more than as a friend. She really, truly cares about you."

Jess shrugged, pleased by the information Blayne shared, but frustrated that Doris refused to acknowledge what was between them. "I still don't know what I can do to change her mind."

Blayne sat quietly for a while, drinking his coffee. Suddenly, he looked over at Jess with a broad grin. "Do you have a red shirt? Some white socks you don't mind ruining?"

Jess looked at him like he was crazy. "I do. What have you got in mind?"

"What if you…"

Blayne left an hour later while Jess made himself comfortable in his recliner. He opened a book he'd started reading, but was so distracted, listening for the sound of Doris's car, he'd read the same page five times before he gave up and stared out the window.

It wasn't more than twenty minutes after Blayne left that he watched Doris speed up his driveway. He heard the brakes squeal when she slammed on them at the back of the house. He listened as she charged up the back steps and opened the kitchen door.

"Jess? Jess, where are you?" she called as her footsteps clicked across the kitchen floor.

"In here," he said, forcing himself to sound tired, maybe even a little weak.

Doris breezed into the room, a basket of food in one hand and her gloves in the other. "Are you okay? Blayne made it sound like you were practically dying."

She set the basket on the coffee table, stuffed her gloves in her pocket, then reached out to feel his forehead with the back of her hand. "You do feel a little warm. Are you getting sick? What's wrong?"

"Oh, nothing. I don't want to be a bother," he

said, making a concentrated effort to get out of the chair.

"No, you sit right there. I'll put your food on a tray and bring it to you. Do you want tea? Milk? Some coffee? Maybe you should have juice if you're coming down with something. Is your stomach upset? Are you coughing? Should I call the doctor?"

Jess swallowed down a smile and shook his head. "Milk would be fine and no, I'm not sick, just a little tired." That part wasn't a lie. He'd lingered far too long outside this morning, then he and Blayne had spent an hour plotting to bring about this very scenario. It had taken them both digging through Jess's clothes to find a red shirt that would ruin a whole load of white socks before they stuffed everything in the washing machine together. He could do with a few minutes of sitting down to rest, but not because he was about to start knocking on death's door.

He had no idea what Blayne had said to his grandmother, but whatever it was, he'd have to thank him for it later. Right now, he had to convince Doris he still needed her help even if what he wanted was her companionship, friendship, and affection.

"I'll be right back," she said, bustling into the kitchen with the basket. The scent of her, something that had always made him think of cozy winter evenings spent in an English estate library while being tantalized by an exotic woman, lingered in her wake. He sniffed deeply, letting the intoxicating fragrance fill his nose.

Julia had once said something about Doris being the only woman she'd known who could carry off that particular perfume so perfectly. Too bad he couldn't recall the name of it. All he knew, at that moment, was how enticing he found it. And Julia was right. It was perfect for Doris. In spite of the scent that was made for a woman, not a girl, it held a classic, elegant appeal in the undertones that continued to waft around him.

Before he could inhale again, Doris reappeared with a tray she set across his lap. "Blayne said you've hardly eaten. Are you not hungry or just having trouble cooking? What can I do to help?"

"I really don't want to be a bother to you, Doris. Why don't you sit down and keep me company while I eat this wonderful meal?" Jess gave her an imploring look that got her to sit on the couch for five whole minutes as he dove into the best thing he'd eaten in a week, since Doris had declared him well enough to take care of himself and stopped coming to see him.

The roast was so tender it fell apart at the touch of his fork. The dinner roll was soft and light, slathered with butter and homemade blackberry jam. Mashed potatoes, smothered with gravy, and carrots cooked to the exact tenderness he preferred rounded out the meal.

"Is there any housework you need help with? How about laundry?"

"Oh, I put a load in earlier. I'll stick it in the dryer later," he said, glancing over his shoulder in the direction of the kitchen. The laundry room was just off the kitchen down a short hallway.

Doris hopped up and headed that way. Jess cringed when he heard her startled exclamation over his ruined clothes. To make it look like he hadn't done it on purpose, he'd even thrown in one of his good white shirts.

"Jess Milne! Do you not have the sense God gave a dead dog? You know better than to put a red shirt in with a load of white clothes. Look at this. Ruined! Your shirt and socks are ruined!"

She held a handful of wet socks and his once-white shirt out to him. They were streaked various shades of pink. Blayne had added a squirt of red food coloring to the load of laundry from a bottle they'd found in the back of a drawer where Julia had always kept supplies she used for decorating cakes and cookies. Evidently, that squirt had done the job of whatever his red shirt hadn't accomplished. He'd have to order more socks because there was no way he was running around in pink striped ones.

"They are pink aren't they?" he said in a weary tone. "I'm sorry." For added dramatic flair, he pushed back his plate and sighed dejectedly.

Doris instantly stopped glaring at him and patted his arm then nudged his plate toward him again. "You eat every bite of that supper, Jess. I'll take care of the laundry. With a little work, I might be able to get these white again."

"Oh, don't worry about it, Doris. The boys can use those for rags out in the shop."

When she returned to the laundry room, Jess hurried to finish his meal, gulped his milk, then sat back in the chair, doing his best to look ill. In a flash of inspiration, he turned on a heating pad he sometimes used when his back ached and held it against his forehead.

By the time he heard Doris's footsteps coming through the kitchen, he was about to break into a sweat. He turned off the heat pad and dropped it behind his chair then leaned back and did his best to appear sick.

"Jess, you look terrible. What do you need?" Doris asked, bending over him and pressing her cheek to his forehead. "My gracious! You're burning up. Come on, I'll take you to the emergency room."

"No. There's no need for that." Maybe he'd done too good of a job of giving himself a fever. Having her bend over him like that had certainly increased his temperature more than he'd expected. "I'm sure I'll be fine in the morning. I probably just need to rest a bit."

"You lean back and I'll bring you a glass of water." She took the tray off his lap and Jess pushed back his recliner, remaining in it while Doris fussed over him. When he thought he couldn't stand any more of it, she sat down on the couch and began talking about things happening in town.

She discussed practicing with the church choir for the upcoming performance of *A Christmas Carol*. He would have laughed at her descriptions of some of the things happening at the rehearsals, but a man on his deathbed wouldn't be quite as humored as Jess felt.

After an hour, he thought about confessing the truth to Doris. Suddenly, she got to her feet, walked over to him and kissed him lightly on the mouth. Before Jess could gather his wits enough to pull her into his arms, she straightened and brushed a hand over his stubbly cheek. "You get a good night's rest and I'll check on you tomorrow. If you need anything tonight, you just call and we'll be right over."

"Thanks for being such a good friend, Doris," he said in a weak voice. Maybe he ought to ask Mary McKay if he could audition for the play next year since he was doing a good job of acting tonight.

Guilt pricked at him as Doris gathered her things and left, but not enough he wouldn't do the same thing tomorrow. If a state of helplessness kept her coming to see him, then so be it. He'd be the most helpless, pathetic man she'd ever encountered.

Four days later, Jess concluded Blayne was the stupidest human who ever lived. It was his idiotic idea for Jess to pretend to be weak and in need of care so Doris would spend time with him. At first it seemed like a brilliant plan. Then the realization set in that he couldn't do anything with Doris because she'd basically ordered him to stay quiet and rest until he felt better.

He couldn't exactly tell her he felt great. In fact, his knee was almost back to normal. Another week or two, and the doctor told him he could get back to work on the ranch. But forced to spend so much time sitting while faking a weak constitution was setting him back physically in his recovery.

Frustrated, he drove over to see Blayne when he knew Doris was in town at choir practice.

"What are you doing here?" Blayne asked when he got out of his pickup near the shop. It appeared Blayne and one of the hired hands had dismantled the old John Deere tractor yet again.

"You've got to help me fix this thing with Doris."

"I thought she was back to spending a lot of time with you." Blayne gave him a confused look as he wiped his greasy hands on a rag. "Isn't that what you wanted her to do?"

"Yes. No. I mean…" Jess growled and yanked off his hat, forking his hands through his hair. "That woman's got me so tied in knots I can't think straight. But this pretending to be a sick weakling is messing with my knee. I can't heal if I spend all day sitting in my recliner pretending I've got one foot in the grave."

When Blayne started chuckling, Jess had to tamp down the urge to pop him in the nose.

"Let's go on up to the house and see if we can think of a way to get you out of this mess. Brooke asked me to haul all the tree ornaments out of the garage today. How about you help me with that while we talk?"

"Okay." Jess followed him to the house.

After considering and rejecting any number of ideas, Blayne threw up his hands in exasperation. "I don't know what you want me to do, Jess. I want Grams to be happy, but you two have got to work through this without anyone else meddling in it going forward. You can't come on too strong with Grams, but if you can figure out a way to make her think it's her idea to spend time with you it might work. Pretend you've had a miraculous recovery from whatever ailed you and ask her to go do something with you."

Jess set the last tub of decorations in the Grundy living room and glanced at the clock on the wall. Doris would be home soon and he needed to leave before she caught him there with Blayne.

"Are you sure you don't mind me wanting to court your grandma?" Jess asked as Blayne walked out with him to his pickup.

"Nope. Not a bit. My main concern is her happiness, but I sure wouldn't mind having you as an official family member. You've always been like an uncle or grandfather to me, Jess. You know that."

"I do, son. Thank you." Jess gave him a bear hug then climbed in his pickup and left.

By the time he got home, he landed on an idea to get Doris to spend time with him while doing something fun. When she arrived at the house an hour and a half later, he sat at the kitchen table, prepared to put his plan into action.

"What have you got there?" Doris asked as she stepped inside and set a foil-covered plate in front of him.

Jess held up a Christmas ornament Janet had made when she was about six or seven. The bedraggled clothespin reindeer was missing one googly eye and half a pipe-cleaner antler looked like it had been gnawed by a mouse. Julia couldn't bring herself to throw it away but had said the thing was too ugly to hang on the tree. It had taken Jess forty-five minutes to find it, but he hoped it would serve him well in his devious endeavors.

"Janet made this when she was just a little thing. I remember the day she brought it home from school. She was so proud of her reindeer. Julia made over it so, proclaiming it the finest reindeer she'd ever seen, then together they hung it on the tree right in front where Janet could proudly admire it." Jess forced himself to sound maudlin and on the verge of breaking down. "It's been years since I've had a tree. I usually spend Christmas with Janet, Steve, and the kids at their place, but this year..." He let his voice trail off. "It doesn't matter anyway."

Doris sniffled and yanked a tissue from the pocket of her coat, dabbing at her eyes and nose. "We'll get you a tree. Tomorrow."

"A tree? What would I do with a tree? I'm not sure I could decorate it all by myself, although it sure would be nice to smell that Christmassy scent." Jess continued staring at the ornament in his hand, shoulders slumped in a pose meant to look careworn.

"Tomorrow, right after lunch, we'll go pick out a tree at the lot in town. No arguments," Doris slipped off her coat, and turned to get Jess a glass of milk.

He quickly hid his smile and swallowed down the urge to shout out his triumph.

Chapter Nine

"Well, look at that," Jess said, pointing to the marquee at the Esmerelda Theater.

Doris glanced out the window of Jess's pickup and smiled. "Oh, *Miracle on 34th Street*. I've always loved that movie."

Jess pulled around the corner and parked the pickup. "Let's go see it."

Doris saw something glimmering in his eyes that had been absent for a long time. She couldn't tell him no, even if she wanted to, which she didn't. Normally, she was so busy with holiday preparations she hardly had time to blink. This year, though, she was more interested in spending time with people she cared about than making sure every decoration at home was set out just so. Besides, Blayne and Brooke were perfectly capable of seeing to anything she let slide.

"Come on, slowpoke. I'll race you inside," Doris said, hopping down from Jess's pickup and hurrying around the back to try to reach the ticket booth first.

In spite of his healing knee, Jess beat her there and purchased two tickets. After buying popcorn, M&Ms, and beverages, they made their way into the theater and found seats far enough back Jess wouldn't have to crane his neck to see the screen.

Once they'd removed their coats and settled into the seats, Doris dumped her box of candy into the popcorn.

"Why are you contaminating my popcorn with your candy?" Jess asked, digging a handful of golden, buttery kernels from the tub he held between them.

"Because it makes both of them taste better. Try it and you'll see."

Jess gave her a dubious look, but ate the popcorn and quickly filled his hand again.

Doris sipped her water then picked up a few kernels at a time, randomly finding a piece of candy in her hand.

The lights dimmed and flickering images began rolling across the screen. An hour into the movie, Doris leaned her head against Jess's arm and sighed contentedly. She glanced up at him at the same time he looked down at her. He smiled and kissed her nose before looking back at the screen.

If Doris had been sixteen, she might have batted her eyelashes and vowed to never wash her nose again. As it was, she considered what might happen if she offered Jess a little flirtatious encouragement.

She grinned, thinking of his efforts the past week to get her to come see him. He no more needed her help than he needed a third eye in the smack dab middle of his forehead. It took her less than five minutes after she arrived at Jess's house the day Blayne came home claiming their neighbor was nearly on his deathbed to deduce she'd been played.

The reason why her grandson was conspiring with Jess had crossed her mind multiple times, but she was enjoying herself too much to dig for an answer.

When Jess had truly needed her help, she'd felt purposeful and needed. Once he could drive himself and no longer required assistance at home, she felt useless. Brooke and Blayne managed quite well without her, even if they both claimed they couldn't survive a week without her at the ranch.

At any rate, she was glad to have someone who needed her, or at least made a grand pretense of needing her. Jess had gone to so much effort to make her feel necessary to his recovery that she tamped down her first inclination to accuse him of faking illness just to get her to visit him.

Yesterday, when he'd been going on and on about a Christmas tree, she'd decided he may have started out using it as another excuse to keep her close, but she'd seen the emotion in his eyes and heard it in his voice as he held up Janet's pathetic little clothespin reindeer.

Doris knew exactly what he meant, how he felt, because she had a whole box of things she'd saved that her son had made and another full of treasures Blayne had created. Brooke would no doubt love to have both of them someday. For now, the boxes were safely tucked in the back of Doris's closet.

The final credits were rolling before Doris acknowledged how glorious it felt to have Jess's arm around her shoulders. He'd slipped it there thirty minutes into the movie. He felt so good and strong, and so comfortable, she didn't want to move.

When the theater lights came on, she shifted away from him and gathered their trash then picked up her coat.

"Thank you for bringing me to this, Jess. I'd forgotten how fun it was to see this old movie on a big screen."

"Didn't you and Glen ever come to see Christmas movies?" Jess asked, taking her coat from her and holding it while she slipped it on.

"No. We were always so busy with the ranch and other obligations there just wasn't ever time." Doris picked up the popcorn tub with their garbage inside while Jess tugged on his coat. "What about you and Julia? Did you ever bring her?"

Jess nodded. "We used to set aside one day before Christmas just for fun. We'd come to town early, get our shopping done for each other, eat lunch, then wander through some of the stores and buy things for Janet and her family. We'd catch whatever movie was playing, eat dinner out, and then look at lights on our way home."

"That sounds like a wonderful way to spend a day." Doris wished Glen had made more time for fun. He'd always been so driven and hardworking, she often had to remind him that time to rest and play was important, too.

"Shall we go find a tree?" Jess asked, holding out his arm to Doris after she tossed their garbage in a trash can, and they headed toward the door.

"Absolutely. If you ask nicely, I might even be coerced into helping you decorate it."

At the tree lot, Jess would have taken the first tree they came to, but Doris made him walk with her up and down the rows of trees. There were noble firs, Douglas firs, grand firs, white pine, and Scotch pine.

"This one," Doris blurted, fingering a Frasier fir and inhaling a deep breath. The scent was fabulous and the tree was perfectly proportioned.

Jess took a whiff of the tree's aromatic perfume and nodded. "I'll get someone to put a fresh cut on the bottom and stick it in a tree stand."

While he walked off in the direction of what appeared to be the area where one paid for trees, Doris stared at him in disbelief. He'd not even glanced at the price tag, which was quite ridiculous in her opinion. She'd always wanted a Frasier fir, but Glen had told her they were too expensive, even though they could well afford it. His mother had always liked a white pine, so that's what they always had, too. Since he'd been gone, Doris had invested in a high-quality artificial tree she generally put up the day after Thanksgiving and didn't take down until all the confetti from New Year's Eve had been swept up.

Would Jess really buy the expensive tree just

because she said he should? When he returned with a lot attendant who hefted the tree and carried it off to make a fresh cut on the trunk, Doris grabbed Jess's arm.

"We could find a less expensive tree."

He merely shrugged and placed his hand on her back, guiding her through the maze of trees. "I like the way that one smelled and it's pretty."

"But, Jess, we could get a Douglas fir. It would smell good and cost less..."

He stopped and glanced down at her. "It's just a tree, Doris, not a Cadillac. I think you chose well. Now, are we gonna stand out here freezing our toes or go pay for that tree and take it home? I even hauled in all the ornaments this morning and left them in the living room."

"Let's go home," Doris said, giving him a slightly bewildered smile. For more than fifty years, the Rockin' G Ranch had been her home. However, lately Jess's place felt more like home to her. She didn't want to think about why that was. There'd be time enough for that later.

Right now, she had a gorgeous tree to decorate with the help of a very handsome man.

Doris sat at the kitchen table, toying with a spoon while Blayne kissed his wife goodbye.

He tugged on his insulated coveralls and picked

up his hat, then pecked Doris on the cheek. "You two girls have a great day."

"I won't be home for lunch, sweetie. You are on your own," Doris called after him as he hurried out into the cold.

"Are you heading over to see Jess again today?" Brooke asked as she loaded the breakfast dishes into the dishwasher. She glanced over at Doris. "Grams, you're awfully quiet. Is everything okay?"

Doris shrugged. She felt… oh, she didn't know exactly how to explain it or describe it. She felt like a girl in love for the first time. She felt like a wicked woman, secretly betraying her husband. She felt like soaring and crawling all at the same time. How could one feel invigorated and vibrantly alive while wanting to curl up in a ball and weep until there were no tears left?

The emotions warring inside her were about to get the best of her and she didn't know who to talk to. She couldn't share her troubles with any of the women at her book club. She certainly couldn't discuss anything with her grandson because he clearly was in cahoots with Jess. She hated to bother Brooke with her worries.

In the past, when something was eating at her, she would have gone to Jess and Julia. After Julia passed away, she'd still found Jess to be a good sounding board. He'd always offered a listening ear and gave her good feedback.

Since he was at the center of her current inner turmoil, she couldn't very well march inside his house and ask him what she should do.

Brooke sat down beside her and placed a hand over Doris's. "What is it, Grams? What can I do to help you?"

"I'm just being a silly old woman, honey. It's nothing you need to be concerned with."

Brooke smiled. "Try me."

Doris looked at the lovely woman, saw the compassion in her gaze and the warmth in her smile. Before she could stop herself, words began tumbling out. "Jess Milne has quite nearly turned my head, and I don't know whether I should keep running or let him catch me. The past few days have been so wonderful. I feel like a girl again, but when I glance in the mirror, there's a wrinkle-faced old woman who looks frighteningly like my grandmother staring back at me."

Brooke remained quiet, listening attentively.

Doris absently traced the lines of the plaid pattern of the tablecloth with her index finger, unable to meet Brooke's gaze. "I just wish I looked more like I feel inside."

"And how do you feel inside?" Brooke asked.

"Like I'm young and carefree and my whole life is ahead of me. Jess makes me feel so alive. I know it is utter nonsense," Doris sighed. "Then there's part of me that feels like I've lived two lifetimes and to even consider welcoming Jess's attention is a blatant betrayal to Blayne's granddaddy."

"I know Blayne doesn't feel that way and you shouldn't either. He's mentioned several times how much he admires Jess. And I think he's quite a catch, Grams. Not only is he handsome for a man his age, or any age for that matter, he's a kind, gentle man. And he adores you." Brooke gave her hand a squeeze. "Do you really want to change your look?"

Doris hadn't really given it any thought, but she immediately liked the idea. "I think I do."

"Get your things and meet me in my car in fifteen minutes." Brooke raced to finish cleaning up the breakfast dishes then ran from the room.

Doris hastened to her room, combed her hair, brushed her teeth, and changed into the clothes she planned to wear when Jess picked her up to take her into town. He'd asked her to have lunch with him and help him choose gifts for his hired men to go with the cash bonuses he planned to give them. He promised to stay in town while Doris took care of a few errands, then drive her home afterward.

Now, it looked like she'd be heading to town with Brooke. She had no idea what the girl had planned, but she was clearly up to something.

Doris yanked on her coat, grabbed her gloves and purse, then hurried out to Brooke's vehicle.

"Where are we going, honey?" Doris asked as Brooke turned onto the highway and headed toward Romance.

"You'll see when we get there." Brooke gave her a broad smile and cranked up the local radio station that was playing Christmas music.

Rather than drive to her studio, Brooke turned down a different street and parked in front of the hairdresser's shop Doris had gone to for years.

"What are we doing here?" Doris asked.

Brooke hopped out of the vehicle and jogged

around to open Doris's door. "Changing your look, Grams. Are you gonna chicken out?"

Doris squared her shoulders and raised her chin. "Lead on, darling."

An hour later, Doris gawked at the mirror, unable to believe the image staring back belonged to her.

"Oh, Grams!" Brooke hugged her shoulders as she stood behind her, smiling in the mirror. "You look like one of those glamorous stars from the golden days of Hollywood."

Doris put a hand to the chunky curls surrounding her face that were now a light shade of blond instead of white. Just the change in her hair color made her feel twenty years younger. From the way everyone in the shop was gaping and grinning, it appeared she looked that way, too.

The stylist had cut a few layers in Doris's hair and curled it. The curls were then loosened until they softly framed her face — a face sporting more makeup than Doris had ever worn in her life.

"You really like it?" Doris asked, touching the soft curls again. She'd forgotten what she'd looked like without a halo of white hair surrounding her head.

"I love it, Grams. You look amazing." Brooke took her hand and pulled her out of the chair. "But we aren't done yet."

"We aren't?" Doris asked, as she slipped on the coat Brooke held for her. When she took out her wallet to pay, Brooke gently pushed it back in her purse.

"Consider this part of my Christmas gift to

you."

"No, honey. That's too much. I'll…"

"Please, Grams?" Brooke gave her an imploring look. "You and Blayne are the only family I have. Let me spoil you a bit."

Doris hugged her, forcing her tears away as Brooke paid the bill then the two of them stepped outside.

"A new look isn't complete without a new outfit. I know just the place." Brooke held open the door to her SUV and Doris hurried inside.

A few minutes later, they parked behind Brooke's shop. Brooke wrote a note and stuck it on the door in case anyone came looking for her, then escorted Doris across the street and down the block to the dress shop.

They spent an hour going through every piece of clothing that was in Doris's size. She tried on everything Brooke handed to her in the dressing room.

"How about this one?" Doris asked, stepping out of the dressing room and striking a pose that made Brooke laugh.

"Grams! That is it. That's the one. You have to have that dress and I saw a pair of shoes…" Brooke raced off to find a pair of matching shoes with kitten heels. "Try these on," she said, holding out the shoes to Doris.

Doris slipped them on her feet, loving the way they looked and completed the outfit.

"Oh, you look amazing, Grams!"

"You really do look wonderful, Mrs. Grundy," the salesgirl said. "That outfit looks as though it was made for you."

Doris gave herself a studying look in the full-length mirror. The wrap-style gown was simple in design, but the luxurious fabric glided over her curves and accented the fact she'd kept in good shape all these years. The piece of shapewear the salesgirl insisted she wear assisted in giving her a nice silhouette as it lifted and smoothed her form. A slim black belt encircled her waist while long sleeves provided a bit of elegant coverage. The neckline was square, not too low. And the deep sapphire hue perfectly matched the color of her eyes.

In spite of her head shouting, "What have you done?" her heart applauded the changes.

"I'll take it," Doris said, smiling at Brooke and the salesgirl.

"The dress? Shoes? The three other outfits you liked?" Brooke asked.

"All of it," Doris said with a laugh.

"Yes!" Brooke said, and gave her an exuberant hug. "Are you still planning to meet Jess for lunch?"

Doris nodded, pleased by the way she looked in the mirror, especially with Brooke hugging her around the shoulders and giving her a big smile. "I called and let him know to meet here in town instead of picking me up at the ranch."

"That's great. I think you should wear that dress for your lunch date."

"Oh, it's not a date, honey. It's just Jess."

Brooke gave her a knowing look as she raised an expressive eyebrow. "Whatever you say, Grams.

I still think you should wear that dress, though. And I think you should get that other dress you liked, too."

"I will, then." Doris started to head back into the dressing room, but Brooke removed the tag on the dress and gathered the rest of the clothes she planned to purchase.

"I'll take these up to the counter for you."

Doris started to protest, but then nodded once. She returned to the dressing room, fully intending to change back into the clothes she'd worn to town, but she looked in the mirror again, ran her hand down the front of the silky fabric of the dress and decided to wear it. She wondered if Jess would notice the change in her hair or attire.

Annoyed her thoughts continually turned to him, she tried to redirect them, but they just came back around to Jess.

"Oh, what could it hurt, for one day?" she whispered.

Excitement began to stir inside her, swirling through her veins and she suddenly wanted to laugh and dance and enjoy the wonder of being so fully alive in that moment.

Instead, she folded the clothes she'd worn to town, grabbed her coat, purse, and shoes, and headed to the cash register where the salesgirl stuffed her purchases inside a large bag.

"Here, Mrs. Grundy. Let me take those things from you," the girl offered, tucking her shoes and clothes in another bag.

"What do I owe you?" Doris asked, starting to take out her wallet.

"It's all taken care of, Mrs. Grundy," the girl said, glancing at Brooke.

"I'm spoiling you today, Grams. Remember?" Brooke smiled at her and ignored Doris's protests. Brooke took the coat Doris held and helped her slip it on then glanced at her watch. "Come on back to the studio with me until it's time for you to meet Jess. We can have a cup of coffee or tea while you wait and I'll show you my latest project."

"Sure, darling, and thank you," Doris said, picking up one of the bags while Brooke carried the rest out the door.

They returned to Blown Away where Brooke set Doris's bags of clothes in her SUV. She came back inside and made cups of peppermint tea for them both, then they sat down at the worktable and Doris looked at some new pieces Brooke had made.

She had clear glass balls that were so iridescent, they looked like bubbles. Doris touched one, almost expecting it to pop like a bubble would.

"Honey, these are glorious!" Doris exclaimed, amazed by the woman's creativity.

"Thanks, Grams. I thought I'd hang them on fishing line in the display window, so they look like they're floating."

"That's a brilliant idea." Doris smiled as she picked up a small bubble and held it up to the light. "What else have you been working on?"

Brooke showed her a vase that was dark green on the bottom and faded to a soft mint hue at the top where varying shades of pink glass roses rested around the rim.

Doris studied the creation from several angles.

She had no idea how Brooke created it, but she held no doubt it would sell quickly. "It's amazing what you can do with glass, darling."

"I just have fun with it, Grams. Want to see what I made Blayne?"

Doris grinned. "Of course!"

"I had to try three times to get it just right," Brooke said, removing a wrapped object from a heavy cardboard box lined with tissue. She set it on the worktable, removed the wrapping and stepped back. "What do you think?"

"I think he'll love it," Doris said, tracing her finger over one of the horses that appeared to be running right off the lid of an amber-toned glass box.

"You really think so?" Brooke asked, sounding uncertain. "I thought he could keep his good watch and the one pair of cufflinks he owns in it instead of tossing them in a drawer."

"He'll love anything you make, Brooke, but he'll truly cherish this."

The bell above the door jangled, letting them know Brooke had a customer. While Brooke went out front, Doris carefully rewrapped Blayne's gift and tucked it back in the box. She finished her tea, used Brooke's bathroom, and spent a few minutes reapplying the lipstick she'd purchased at the beauty shop then gave her nose a quick dusting of powder.

She returned to the workroom, pulled on her coat and strolled out front. Brooke's customer had just left and Brooke was rearranging a display near the front counter.

"Are you heading off to lunch?" Brooke asked as Doris walked over and gave her a long hug.

"I am, darling. Thank you so much for this morning's makeover. I feel so different, it's kind of scary."

Brooke returned her hug then kissed her cheek. "You look like a million bucks, Grams. Just enjoy it. Are you still planning to spend the afternoon with Jess?"

"Yes, I think so. If I need a ride home, I'll give you a call."

"Okay. I'll be here until five. And don't forget, I promised to make dinner tonight, so if you get home before I do, no cooking for you this evening."

"All right, but I feel like I should do something to pay for all you've done for me this morning."

Brooke shook her head. "No, Grams. It was my pleasure to buy a few things for you. You've been so good to me ever since I first visited the Rockin' G. It's my turn to do something for you. Have fun with Jess. You have to promise to tell me what he says when he sees you. I bet he drops his teeth."

Doris laughed and opened the door. "Now that would be something. Have a wonderful afternoon, darling."

The air outside held a frosty nip. Doris snuggled into the warmth of her coat as she hurried to the restaurant where she said she'd meet Jess. Delicious aromas floated on the air and she realized she was hungry. She saw Jess's pickup parked out front as she rushed inside the warmth of the restaurant.

He sat at a table facing the door, so Doris

smiled at the hostess and breezed past her.

"I hope you haven't been waiting long," she said, slipping off her coat and setting it with her purse on a chair then turning to smile at Jess.

He rose to his feet and stared at her open-mouthed, as though he couldn't quite believe what he was seeing.

A giggle rolled out of Doris before she could contain it. Brooke might have been right about him dropping his teeth if Jess had worn false chompers. Since they were all his own, he merely looked as though he'd had the air knocked out of him and waited for it to return.

Abruptly, his mouth snapped shut, but his eyes remained wide, full of surprise, as he stepped around the table and pulled out her chair.

"Doris? Is that really you?" he whispered in her ear, giving her a hug that lasted far longer than she deemed appropriate in such a public place.

"It's me. Who'd you think it was?" she gave him an admonishing look as she sat down in the chair he held for her. She wondered when he'd grown six extra arms, because his hands seemed to be everywhere at once: brushing her arm, caressing her shoulder, skimming across her cheek, touching her hair.

"Jess," she admonished quietly. "That is enough. Sit down."

"Whatever you say, Doris," he said in a tone she'd never heard him use. His voice sounded husky, intimate, as he spoke her name.

Unsettled, and wondering what kind of trouble Brooke had talked her into, Doris snapped open the menu in front of her and hid behind it until the server came to take their orders. When she left, Doris had no choice but to face Jess. He appeared almost stupefied as he continued staring at her.

"Are you going to say something, you old goat, or do you plan to keep ogling me like some sort of deranged sicko?" Doris gave him a coy look followed by a dazzling smile.

Jess blinked, then blinked again. He reached for a glass of ice water the server set on the table and gulped down half of it before he blinked a third time. Finally, he cleared his throat, started to speak, then closed his mouth. The second time he tried and failed to utter anything, Doris couldn't hold back another giggle.

"What's gotten into you, Jess? Are you feeling poorly again?"

He shook his head and a grin slowly spread across his face. He reached across the table, captured one of her hands and lifted it to his lips, kissing her fingers. "You look beautiful, Doris. Not that you don't always look nice, but I hardly recognized you. If I hadn't known better, I would have thought I was seeing a version of you from twenty years ago. You've obviously had a busy morning."

She tugged her fingers from his and settled her hands on her lap. The heat flickering in his stormy gray eyes made her a little frightened and uncertain. If she'd wanted to get Jess's attention, she'd certainly hit the mark. He didn't seem able to take his eyes off her and the attention was more than she knew how to handle.

"Brooke did all this," Doris said, waving a hand in front of her. "I mentioned wanting a change and the next thing I knew, I was sitting in a chair at the salon and no longer had white hair. I'd forgotten what I looked like when I had blond hair."

"You were always a looker, Doris. Always. When Glen married you, half the men in Romance mourned the fact you were off the market."

Doris scowled. "You make me sound like a cow at an auction."

Jess smirked. "Not at all. Just a beautiful woman any man would be fortunate to know."

She blushed at his comment, aware he wasn't tossing out a line, but speaking from his heart.

He leaned back and gave her clothes a studying glance. "New outfit?"

"Yes. More of Brooke's help. I think I tried on every outfit at the dress shop this morning."

"Brooke has great taste," Jess said, then fell silent when the server brought their meals. They spoke of the shopping Jess wanted to do, the community performance of *A Christmas Carol* tomorrow, where Doris would sing with the choir, and the gifts Doris had hidden at Jess's house for Brooke and Blayne.

When they finished eating, Jess paid the bill and helped Doris with her coat, touching her far more than was necessary for the simple task.

"What is wrong with you?" Doris whispered as he placed a hand to the small of her back and walked her outside and over to his pickup.

He opened the front passenger door and helped her in, his hands lingering on her waist. He didn't speak until he'd climbed behind the wheel and started it, waiting for warm air to blow through the vents.

Jess reached over and fingered a curl that bobbed against her cheek. "You take my breath away, Doris. Don't blame a man for being unable to keep his hands to himself when you look like a movie star."

Heat soaked her cheeks and she turned away, looking out the window. Part of her wanted to slide across the seat, wrap her arms around Jess's neck, and give him a kiss.

The other part considered jumping out of his pickup and running to Blown Away where she could hide in Brooke's workroom or the apartment upstairs until her granddaughter could take her home.

Jess chuckled then put the truck in gear and pulled into the street.

While they worked on his shopping list for his hired hands, he didn't make any more comments about her appearance or do more than occasionally touch her back or brush her arm. Much to Doris's surprise, they went to a store that carried a large variety of children's toys.

"What are we doing here? Your grandkids are too old for toys like this," she said, shooting a bewildered glance in his direction.

"You'll see," Jess said, then proceeded to fill three shopping carts with gifts. He paid a group of 4-H students who had a gift-wrapping table set up for a fundraiser near the entrance to wrap them all. The kids helped carry the gifts out to his pickup where they piled the backseat full.

After that, Jess took Doris to Sweet Hearts Pastry & Treats.

"Aren't you still full from lunch?" Doris asked as Jess held the door for her and escorted her inside.

"No, I'm not. Shopping for all those toys made me hungry." Jess walked with her to the counter where Savannah Miller helped customers.

Doris perused the selections available then smiled at Savannah when they reached the counter.

"Hello, Savannah. How are you today?" Doris asked as she removed her gloves and unbuttoned her coat.

Savannah offered them a friendly smile. "I'm great, Mrs. Grundy. What brings you both to the bakery this afternoon?"

"We've been busy shopping and are in dire need of sustenance," Jess said with a teasing grin.

Savannah laughed and pointed to a case full of pastries, doughnuts, muffins, and cookies. "You came to the right place. What can I get for you?"

"Hmm, so many delicious-looking options," Doris said glancing from the pastries to intricately decorated cookies. "It's going to be hard to decide." She studied the pretty girl a moment. "Did I see you speaking with Baxter Reid the other night at the tree lighting? I didn't realize he was back in town. Aren't you house-sitting for his grandparents?"

Savannah's shoulders stiffened. "I am and you did see me speak to him. He recently moved back to Romance."

"I see. Didn't he used to antagonize you to no end when you were younger?" Doris questioned, continuing to observe Savannah.

Rather than answer, the young woman forced a smile. "Would you like some hot chocolate? The peppermint is hard to beat."

"We'll take two cups, and how about some sugar cookies?" Jess said, giving Doris a look she couldn't quite interpret, but assumed meant she should cease grilling Savannah about the Reid boy.

"Excellent choice."

While Jess helped Doris remove her coat and the two of them took a seat at a table, Savannah filled mugs with steaming hot chocolate. She carried the drinks, along with their cookies, to the table. "Enjoy the rest of your day," she said, then hurried back to the counter.

Jess and Doris sipped the hot chocolate, devoured the cookies, and discussed how festive the town appeared, bedecked for the holidays. When they finished their refreshments, they walked around the town square, admiring the decorations and thousands of twinkling white lights.

As they neared the towering tree, Jess produced an ornament of a pink pig. "Help me find a place to hang this thing," he said.

"Give it here." Doris held out her hand to him as she looked for a perfect spot for the ornament on the community Christmas tree. "I'm surprised you didn't have Pigtails' name painted on the back of this," Doris said, hanging the ornament on a branch up as high as she could reach."

"What makes you think it's my pig?" he asked with a jaunty grin.

She shook her head and took the hand he held

out to her, following as he led her around the square. When Jess insisted on taking a photo of her in front of the gazebo, she stood stiffly as he snapped a photo.

"Quit holding back, Doris. I know you can do better than that," he said with a teasing gleam in his eye.

She struck a pose similar to the one she'd made at the dress shop. Jess nearly dropped his phone, but he recovered and snapped a few photos.

"I can take a photo of you together, if you like," a young man named Jack Nelson volunteered as he approached them. He worked for the state tourism board, although Doris wasn't sure what he was doing in Romance.

Jess handed his phone to Jack and hurried to stand behind Doris.

She held her breath when he wrapped his arms around her waist and pulled her close. His woodsy, masculine scent filled her nose while the warmth of his big body enveloped her. In that moment, Doris felt lost — undeniably lost to her longing to love this man who was becoming far, far more than a dear friend. Lost to the hope there was more in her future than one lonely day stretched out after another, then another. Lost to the feeling that in Jess's arms was exactly where she wanted and needed to be.

"I think I got something you can use," Jack said, returning Jess's phone to him.

"Thank you, Mr. Nelson," Doris said, giving him a smile as he tipped his head to her then continued on his way.

Jess and Doris strolled back out to the street and past Brooke's shop, then turned and made their way toward his pickup.

Two men stepped out of the hardware store and stopped, then whistled at Doris.

She tossed them a scathing glare while secretly pleased by the attention.

Jess laughed and took her hand in his. "Come on, Miss Glamorpuss, let's deliver those toys." He drove to the hospital where they carried in the toys and left them with a nurse who was apparently sworn to secrecy.

Doris knew someone brought toys to the hospital every year for the children who had to spend Christmas there, but no one ever seemed to know who donated the gifts.

"How many years have you done that?" Doris asked as Jess helped her back inside his pickup.

He shrugged. "Oh, I suppose it's going on close to thirty years. Julia and I started doing it one year when Janet was in the hospital. Remember when her appendix burst and she spent Christmas here?"

Doris nodded, recalling how miserable the girl had been. Janet was convinced Santa wouldn't leave her any presents if she was in the hospital. Doris and Glen had taken Janet a few gifts on Christmas Day to cheer her, but it appeared Santa had visited her, along with the other children who were there.

"I had no idea, Jess. It's so kind that you do this for the children." Doris again found herself at odds in her feelings toward Jess Milne. One moment he was driving her nuts, and the next, she wanted to give him a big hug.

"It's my pleasure to do it." He climbed into the pickup and gave her a long look. "Are you in a rush to get home? Would you have dinner with me?"

"Brooke's cooking dinner tonight, so I'm free as a bird."

"And twice as lovely as one," he muttered as he pulled into traffic and drove them out of town. She had no idea where they were headed. An hour later, he parked in front of an Italian restaurant. "You still like a good plate of ravioli?" he asked.

"I do. I'm surprised you remembered." Doris recalled twice when she and Glen had gone out to dinner with Julia and Jess at this restaurant. One occasion had been Julia's birthday and the second time they were celebrating a loan she and Glen had paid off six months early. They'd hated to borrow money, but they'd had to replace a failed septic system and the cost of it was more than they could pay out-of-pocket at the time. It had been a wonderful evening when they'd gleefully made that final payment and asked Jess and Julia to join them for dinner.

"Let's get inside out of this cold air," Jess said, helping her down from the pickup. He held her hand as they crossed the parking lot and as the hostess showed them to a cozy corner table with a window that looked out on the river. Lights from surrounding businesses and homes glistened on the water.

Doris started to shrug out of her coat, but Jess helped her then waited until she settled herself in the booth before he removed his coat. He tossed both coats on the bench seat beside him then took a seat. A candle in a glass jar and a poinsettia plant added festive flair to the romantic atmosphere.

When she looked over at Jess, he had such an intense look in his eyes she wanted to squirm when his gaze fused to hers.

"Doris, I..."

"I'm Jamie. Thank you for dining with us. I'll be your server this evening," a cheerful young woman said as she greeted them. After taking their orders for beverages and giving them a few moments to decide on what they wanted for dinner, she returned and promised to bring a basket of bread sticks right out.

Sensing Jess was about to say something she wasn't ready to hear, Doris chattered like her life depended on it, even after their meals arrived. She asked if Janet received the box of gifts she'd helped Jess mail last week. She talked about which of his hired hands were going to take a few days off during the holidays. She discussed the play, the decorations in town, and resorted to asking him about Pigtails.

"That little oinker sure liked the toy you brought over the other day," he said, smiling as he cut another bite of lasagna. "Pigtails hasn't escaped once since we put it in her stall.

Doris had found an idea for a toy for pigs online and made one for Tigger. He'd been so entertained with it he'd all but abandoned his ongoing efforts to get out of his pen. Based on the success with Brooke's little escape artists, Doris made one for Pigtails and brought it over a few days earlier. The toy was nothing more than a dowel that ran through empty juice and pop bottles as well as a milk jug. The dowel hung from two boards that had braces on the bottom to keep them upright. Doris had used old scrap wood and a staple gun to make the stands.

Pigtails had been as happy with her toy as Tigger was with his. The little piglet spent hours spinning the bottles around and around, squealing with joy as she played.

"I'm so glad she likes it. Maybe she just needs to keep her mind busy so she doesn't have time to think about sneaking away."

"Maybe she does," Jess said, giving her a look that made her think he was talking about something that had nothing to do with the pig.

Once they finished their meal, which Jess insisted on paying for, they walked outside into the cold.

Their breath made frosty curls above their heads as it lifted in the night air.

"Want to take a walk?" Jess asked, pointing to a path that meandered along the river. Someone had draped so many white lights on the path and over the bushes that it looked like a road to an enchanted fairyland.

"Sure," her mouth said, while her head screamed for her to get in the pickup and demand Jess take her straight home.

Silence surrounded them as they strolled along the path. When they came to a bench, Jess motioned for her to take a seat. He settled close beside her, slipping his arm around her and tucking her against his side. Grateful for his warmth, she tried to ignore how right it felt to be there, to be so near to him.

"Doris, you've about done me in."

She turned and looked at him, having no idea what he meant. "Jess, I…"

He placed his index finger on her mouth, refusing to let her speak. "I thought I'd have a full-fledged heart attack when you walked inside the restaurant at lunch today, looking like you stepped right out of one of those old movies we enjoy watching. You are a beautiful, intelligent, amazing, attractive woman. One I love with all my heart. I've loved you for a long time, Doris. It took years before the pain of losing Julia stopped hurting with every breath I drew in, but a few years ago, I realized the reason I wasn't so mired in grief was because of you. You've been about the best friend I've ever had, and I can't think of anyone I'd rather share what's left of my life with. Doris, you've got to know how much you mean to me, how very much I love you." His eyes glimmered with hope and emotion as he captured her gaze. "Will you please do me the honor of…"

"No, Jess. No." Doris didn't let him finish his proposal, if that was indeed what he planned to ask. As wonderful as the day had been, as much as she'd enjoyed his attention, she couldn't let things go any farther between them. Not when she felt as though being with Jess somehow betrayed Glen. Not when she was sure Jess had suddenly turned so romantic solely because she looked younger, prettier. "I'd like to go home now."

She turned and marched back up the path toward the parking lot. The fast pace she kept made

Jess struggle to keep up with her. He finally gave up and let her race ahead of him. She kept her back to him as he unlocked the pickup, not saying a word as she scrambled inside, pushing his hands away when he attempted to help her.

The entire trip home, she kept her face turned straight ahead, not speaking a single word. Out of the corner of her eye, she saw Jess cast her several worried glances, but he didn't force the issue. Didn't call her a coward, like she knew she deserved.

When he stopped in front of the Rockin' G, Doris opened the door and hustled out before he could unbuckle his seatbelt. "Goodbye, Jess."

Tears streamed down her cheeks as she fumbled with the door and made her way inside. She ignored the questions Brooke and Blayne asked as she rushed to her room and slammed the door, as well as their pleas for her to talk to them.

With a sob, she collapsed on her bed and cried until she thought she'd never stop.

Chapter Ten

"Happy Christmas Eve, Pigtails," Jess said, opening the stall door and leaning over to give the rapidly growing piglet a good back scratch. The piglet grunted and rolled onto her back, enjoying rubs on her tummy.

"Looks like you're the only female interested in any loving from me," he said, petting her for several moments then standing her on her feet before he fed her and refilled her water bowl.

He gave attention to the horses in the barn, checked on a cow the hands had brought in that was acting sickly, then stopped outside the barn to play with the dogs. Unable to find anything else to do and with his knee aching from the cold, he made his way inside the house and removed his outerwear.

Everywhere he looked, he saw Doris. She'd brought a centerpiece of red and white amaryllis for the kitchen table. She'd hung a garland over the window above the kitchen sink.

The cookie jar was full of chocolate cookies with a mint candy right in the center. Jess took a handful of cookies and poured a glass of milk, then made his way into the living room. The fir tree stood in front of the window and filled the house with a scent that brought to mind happy Christmas mornings from his past.

Doris had helped him decorate the tree then artfully arranged several packages beneath it. He knew she'd hid a few there that belonged to Brooke and Blayne. He wondered if she'd come get them or send Blayne to retrieve them. If he felt like venturing over to the Rockin' G, he could deliver them, but he sure didn't want to chance running into Doris.

She'd made it perfectly clear the other night when he'd confessed his feelings for her what she thought about him. He'd even had a ring tucked in his pocket, but she'd cut him off before he could finish his heartfelt proposal.

He'd planned to spend the afternoon with her then whisk her away for a romantic dinner long before she'd called him that morning and said she wanted to meet him in town for lunch instead of riding in with him.

How was he to know she'd spend that morning transforming herself from pretty to gorgeous? He thought he'd reacted as any man might when the woman he loved suddenly appeared looking much different than she had the last time he'd seen her.

In hindsight, he wondered if he'd drooled at

lunch as he kept staring at her. It was hard not to with her hair and face all done up. The dress she wore could have been on a body decades younger for the way it glided around curves he didn't fully realize she still had. And the color of that silky gown had made her eyes shine like jewels — deep blue, rich, and enticing. How was he supposed to resist all that?

He'd been smitten with her before, but seeing her like that had made something spark inside him he'd assumed died with Julia.

He loved Doris for many reasons. She gave him friendship and companionship. She challenged him, frustrated him to the point he wanted to throttle her, yet he found her fascinating, invigorating, and enchanting. He enjoyed talking to her, listening to her share about her family and friends, or ask him for his opinion and advice. The sound of her laughter made him smile. When they got into a verbal sparring match, he felt so alive, it was a marvel electricity didn't spark between the two of them.

And if he wanted to complete the list, he desired Doris. Perhaps it was silly for a man his age to want a woman the way he wanted her, but it was there, all the same. He loved her, in all the ways a man could love a woman, but she'd turned away from him without a word of regret or an opportunity to reason with her stubborn pride or whatever it was that held her back.

He knew she cared about him, too. If he wasn't mistaken, he'd seen love in her eyes many times. Regardless of what she felt, she'd chosen to push him away, again.

Tired of having his love thrown back in his face, he decided it was time to let his dreams of marrying Doris go. Maybe he'd sell the ranch and move closer to Janet. He couldn't abide the thought of living in town, but he could purchase a few acres where he could have a few animals and keep himself busy doing... something.

He could take Pigtails along. The effort to thwart her repeated escape attempts might fill an hour or two of each day.

The last thing he wanted to do was leave Romance, leave the ranch and a home he enjoyed with friends and neighbors he genuinely liked. But what else could he do? He couldn't bear to be around Doris any longer. Short of turning into a recluse and never venturing anywhere he might run into her, moving seemed to be the only other option.

Jess returned to the kitchen, opened a can of soup, and made lunch. He sat at the table and glanced outside, then did a double-take. It was starting to snow.

Imagine that. Snow on Christmas Eve.

It had been years since they'd had a snowy Christmas.

"Well, how about that," he said aloud, watching fluffy flakes drift down from the gunmetal-hued sky.

He switched chairs so he could watch it snow as he ate. After he finished his meal and cleaned up the dishes, he returned to the front room, turned on the tree lights, and settled into his recliner. He turned on the television, flipped through a few programs, then found a channel playing Christmas shows. He watched a holiday movie, chuckling at the antics of Ralphie in *A Christmas Story*, before he fell asleep.

The sound of someone pounding on the door awakened him an hour later.

"Coming," he hollered when the pounding resumed. He swung open the front door to see Blayne standing on the step. "What are you doing over here?"

"Two reasons. I'm sure you heard Chase Lockhart and Izzy Sutton are getting married today."

Jess nodded. "Who hasn't heard that?"

Blayne grinned. "Anyway, with all this snow, I'm going to haul my team along with the old cutter sleigh into town to give them a ride to their wedding, but I wanted to attach bells to the harnesses. Do you have an extra set I can borrow? For the life of me, I can only find one set at home. I can't help but think Grams used them to decorate something, but she's refused to speak to me since yesterday morning."

Jess motioned for Blayne to follow him to the kitchen. "Why is Doris not speaking to you?"

Blayne stared out the window at the snow continuing to fall. "I may have said some things she took exception to hearing."

"Such as?" Jess asked as he pulled on boots and his coat.

"The other night when you dropped her off, she went to her room and refused to speak to either Brooke or me. We could hear her crying her heart out, but she'd locked the door and wouldn't open it. The next day, she barely said a word and kept sniffling. She did go sing with the choir at the play, but when Brooke and I tried to talk to her about what was wrong, all she'd say is 'nothing.' Yesterday morning, after Brooke left for her shop, I wouldn't take 'nothing' as an answer. She finally admitted she thought you were going to propose and explained how she cut you off. I may have shared my thoughts on the subject in a way she didn't completely appreciate. She's got it in that thick head of hers that she's somehow betraying Gramps if she allows herself to admit she's in love with you."

"I don't think she's in love with me or she wouldn't be so determined to keep me away."

Blayne sighed and looked back at Jess. "She's loved you as more than just a friend for a while, even if she won't admit it. I know you feel the same way about her. It's a shame for two people who care about each other as much as the two of you do to not be together. I want Grams to be happy and the happiest I've seen her since Gramps died has been the last few weeks when she's been with you."

"I only wish I could convince your grandmother that we'd be good together. That we aren't betraying Glen or Julia by falling in love again." Jess tugged on gloves and stepped outside. Blayne followed him to the tack room in the barn where he let him choose two matching sets of bells from the many he had hanging there. "What do you suggest I do?"

"Well, after I shared my opinions on the matter

with Grams, yet again, when I stopped in the house a little bit ago she got so mad at me she stormed out of the house. She said she was spending the rest of the holiday at the cabin."

Jess frowned. "That old cabin she and Glen lived in when Doris couldn't stomach more of your great-grandmother's nastiness?"

"That's the one. We keep the power on out there, and there's dry wood stacked on the porch. In fact, there might even be some bottles of water from the last time Brooke and I..." Blayne snapped his mouth shut.

Jess laughed and thumped him on the back. "It's okay, son. I was once a young man with a beautiful bride. Sometimes it's nice to sneak away from everything."

"Yes, sir, it is." Blayne gave him a studying glance. "Perhaps if you go to the cabin, you can claim another beautiful bride. Grams would have a hard time running away from you out there, especially with all this snow. Maybe you can convince her to see things from a different viewpoint."

"Now you're talking, Blayne." Jess walked with him to his pickup.

"I'm hoping you can get her to come back to the house. Brooke and I have a special announcement we want to share with her in the morning. According to rumors I've heard, it's exactly what she asked Santa to bring her this year."

Jess grinned and thumped Blayne on the shoulder. "Congratulations, son. When is the baby due?"

"The end of May. Brooke and I've known for a while, but we wanted to wait to tell Grams for Christmas. You won't say anything to her, will you? I kinda wanted her to be the first to know, but it just seems right to tell you, too."

Jess felt warmth fill his heart. "I'm glad you told me and I won't say a word to your grandmother. I'll act as surprised as anyone when you tell her tomorrow."

Blayne nodded. "Good luck to you. If anyone can talk some sense into her, it's you."

"I hope you're right." Jess pointed toward the house. "Your grandma left some gifts here for you and Brooke. Do you want to take them with you?"

"No. If you can't get her to let you in the cabin, she'll have to come get them later." Blayne gave him an encouraging look. "The best gift I can think of would be to hear that you two are finally going to be together."

"I'll see what I can do. If you run into Santa, put in a good word for me."

"Will do," Blayne said. He waved as he shut the pickup door and then headed down the drive.

Jess tipped his head up and watched the snow steadily fall. Since it began at noon, several inches had accumulated. He walked around, tamping it down beneath his boots. There was plenty for the runners of a sleigh to glide over.

With a plan quickly forming in his mind, he hurried to the shed where he kept equipment they rarely used and pushed open the big door. In the far corner was an old sleigh that had belonged to his grandparents. It made for a romantic, cozy ride on a

141

snowy winter night.

He worked his way around equipment, wondering how he'd get the sleigh pulled out of the shed with so much other equipment in front of it. He'd just yanked off the tarp covering it when he heard the door squeak.

"What are you doing, boss?" Pete asked as he stood in the large doorway.

"Preparing to win the fair lady's heart," Jess quipped, giving the young cowboy a grin.

"Then let me get some help. If you want to use that sleigh, it will take more than me and you to get it dug out before spring." Pete disappeared and soon returned with the three other cowboys who hadn't left for the holiday.

While they unearthed the sleigh, Jess hurried into the house and changed into warmer clothes, tucked a velvet box into a deep pocket inside his coat, and zipped it. He grabbed a stack of blankets and snagged a basket Doris had left behind, filling it with food that could serve as their dinner, then he rushed back outside.

By the time he made it to the shed, the boys had the sleigh out and were using a rag to wipe off thick dust and cobwebs.

Pete helped him catch two horses he used in parades to pull a wagon. The horses spent most of their time grazing in the pasture, but when they were pressed into service they offered a showy presence. Their dark brown coats were covered with snow as Pete and Jess brushed them off then began harnessing them.

"You want one of us to go with you, boss? If

Vic and Bert spook, I don't want you to hurt that knee of yours," Pete said as he fastened sleigh bells around the neck of Bert. He glanced over at Jess and grinned. "Tell me again how the horses got their names?"

"My daughter was on a big history kick when these two were born. She dubbed them Victoria and Albert, after the Victorian queen and her beloved prince." Jess fastened a string of bells around Vic's neck. "So I shortened the names to Vic and Bert"

"Good names for good horses," Pete said, patting Bert's neck as two of the other cowboys quickly fastened the traces.

"Thank you for your help. If all goes well, I'll come back with Mrs. Grundy. If I don't come back at all, it means she's completely broken my heart and I've gone off to end my lonely existence or she's finally killed me and I'm heels up in a snowbank."

Pete shook his head. "That ain't gonna happen, boss. What woman could resist a sleigh ride on Christmas Eve?"

"Let's hope she doesn't prove to be the exception to the rule," Jess said, climbing up in the sleigh. He'd already set in the blankets and basket of food. He'd forgotten just how nice the sleigh looked when it was all polished. He'd had it restored as a Christmas surprise for Julia about thirty years ago, but the creamy leather upholstery looked as though he'd only recently had the work done. The black paint of the sleigh, accented with pinstripes of gold gleamed in the fading light.

"Wait, Jess," Pete said, running to the shop and

returning with a battery operated lantern. "You might need this if you stay out too long."

Jess took the light from him and set it on the floor next to the blankets and basket of food. "Thanks, Pete. That might come in handy later." Jess flipped a blanket over his lap, picked up the reins, and grinned at his men. "Wish me luck!"

"Go get her, boss man!" one of the men yelled and the others cheered.

The horses seemed as eager for an adventure as he felt as they pulled the sleigh across the newly fallen snow. Rather than go out to the road, Jess guided the team past the pond and out toward the pasture that connected to the Grundy's property. From there, it was a short distance to the cabin where he hoped to find Doris.

He was almost to the gate that separated the two properties when the sound of hoof beats pounding behind him made him look back.

"I'll get the gate for you," Pete said as he rode by then hopped down and opened the gate.

The opening was barely wide enough to get the sleigh through, but Jess made it. "Thanks, Pete."

"Good luck, boss," the young man called, then closed the gate.

Jess had no trouble reaching the cabin. By the time he got there, it was almost dusk. Lights glowing from inside the small, snug structure appeared welcoming against the darkening sky.

The horses shook their manes, setting the bells to jingling as he neared the cabin. Suddenly, the door swung open and Doris stepped outside, wearing an afghan as a shawl around her shoulders.

She gaped at the sight of the team and sleigh, her surprise turning to a smile before she realized who drove the horses.

One look at Jess and she spun around, going back inside the cabin and slamming the door. The entire building shuddered from the force of it. Convincing her to marry him wouldn't be an easy task.

Jess stopped the horses outside the cabin, covered the basket of food with the blanket he'd used to cover his lap, and stepped onto the porch of the little house.

"Doris, I'm not leaving until you talk to me, so you might as well open this door," he said loudly, well aware she could hear him. "If I die out here of exposure to the elements, you'll go to your grave knowing my death is because of you."

"Oh, shush, you overdramatic, big-mouthed blowhard and get in here," Doris said, yanking open the door and glaring at him.

"I sure missed you, baby," Jess said, wrapping his arms around her and giving her a hug before she could step away.

"I'm not your baby," she said, but the protest sounded half-hearted at best. She waited a full minute before she pushed against him and he let her go. "What are you doing here?" Her gaze narrowed. "I can only assume my traitorous blabbermouth grandson told you where to find me."

"Blayne did stop by and mentioned your whereabouts," Jess said, closing the door behind him and removing his coat.

Doris raised an eyebrow at him. "You might as

well leave that on because you aren't staying."

"Well, neither are you. Do you really want Blayne and Brooke to remember this as the Christmas you threw a hissy fit because everything and everyone wasn't fitting into the little boxes of your ordered world?"

"I'm not throwing a hissy fit, you... you..." Doris appeared to search for a word to describe him and couldn't find one adequately detestable. She walked across the room and stared out the window that overlooked a pasture full of Angus cattle huddled together against the snow.

Jess took off his hat and set it with his coat on the straight-backed chair near the door. "You're lucky I've got a tough ol' hide that isn't easy damaged by the barbs you keep throwing my way. Instead of fighting me, why don't you try letting me love you, Doris? You and I both know it's what you really want."

She turned around, eyes brimming with tears and shook her head. "How would you know what I want, what I feel?"

"Because I know how I feel, the questions I've dealt with." He sighed and moved closer to her, but didn't touch her, didn't reach out like he felt such an urge to do. "When I first realized I cared for you, Doris, not just as a friend or neighbor, but a woman who set my heart to thumping like a drum, I felt like I'd cheated on Julia. Like I'd somehow betrayed her and the beautiful life we had together. It took me a while to come around to the realization the betrayal was in holding so tight to my memories and the vows I made to her that I was forgetting that she'd want me to be happy. Whether happiness was from being alone or with a good woman who makes my soul smile, she'd give me her blessing if she could. And I know Glen would do the same. You aren't betraying him or your vows, or whatever you've convinced yourself you're doing by allowing yourself to love again."

Jess took a deep breath and studied her. "You're afraid, Doris Grundy. You're afraid of loving me and losing me and that's what is holding you back more than anything else. We all have to die sometime. I could walk out that door and die five minutes later. We could both be struck down standing here in this cabin. We might live to be a hundred and ten and terrorize Blayne and Janet and their families for thirty more years."

The barest hint of a smile appeared on her quivering lips.

"The question you need to answer is this: are you willing to miss out on what might be because you are a coward?"

She scowled at him and turned back around to look outside. "I'm not a coward, Jess Milne. It's just silly for people our age to think they're falling in love. The emotions and longings are impossible to believe."

"Impossible? What's impossible?" he asked, placing his hands on her shoulders and turning her to face him.

"Us. This. Whatever it is between us," she said, motioning between the two of them. "What I feel for you can't be real, can't be possible, because it's just too big, too grand, too much."

He pulled her against his chest and kissed the top of her head. "Why don't you focus some of that amazing energy of yours on thinking of what our future together might be like instead of deciding what we feel for each other is make-believe? Anything is possible if you truly believe with all your heart." He tipped her chin up and smiled at her. "Don't you give up on you and me, Doris. I love you more than I ever dreamed it possible to love another woman after Julia. I need you with every breath I breathe. If you don't know by now how much I love you, then maybe this will clear things up once and for all."

Jess captured her lips with a fervent, driven kiss that said far more than mere words could ever express. Mercy! Kissing this woman was more decadent than he'd imagined. Apparently, passion wasn't something he'd grown too old to feel as he pulled her closer and deepened the kiss.

When her arms slipped around his neck and she whispered his name, he knew he'd won.

"Marry me, Doris. Let me make however many years we have left together as magical as they can be. Say yes, baby."

"Yes, Jess. I'll marry you," she said, kissing him again and holding him so close, he could feel her heart galloping, keeping time to his own.

"When?" he asked, kissing her cheeks, her nose, her neck.

"As soon as we can get a license. How about New Year's Eve?"

"I'll do my best to restrain myself until then," he said, leaning back and waggling his eyebrows suggestively.

"You perverted old coot. I should have left you out in the cold," she said. Although she smacked his chest, the touch was playful and turned into a caress. "You're a handsome, handsome man, Jess Milne, and I can't think of any finer. I do love you, so much."

"I'm glad to hear that." He took the ring box out of his coat pocket, opened the lid and held out the ring nestled on a bed of black velvet. A white gold band, set with diamonds and sapphires glittered in the light shining from the nearby lamp.

"Oh, Jess, it's beautiful." Tears again filled her eyes as Jess took the ring and slid it on her finger.

"I do love you so, Doris." He kissed her sweetly, softly. "Now, what do you say we go for a little sleigh ride then head back to my place. We're too late to make Chase and Izzy's wedding, but we could have a little fun playing Santa over at your house."

"I'd love it, Jess, and I love you."

He helped Doris bundle into her coat then tugged on his own. They turned off the lights then hurried out to the sleigh. Jess had left a blanket on the seat to keep snow from covering it. Doris picked up the blanket and shook off the snow. Once she took a seat and he slid in next to her, he lifted two dry blankets from the stack on the floor and covered their laps, then pointed to the basket of food.

"If you're hungry, I packed a few snacks."

"You thought of everything, didn't you?" She pulled a cookie from a resealable bag and held it out to him before taking one. "Were you so certain you'd convince me to see things your way?"

He kissed her cheek and grinned. "I wasn't leaving here until you did. Besides, Blayne is nearly as determined as I am that we should be together."

"I'm glad you didn't give up, Jess. Thank you for loving me even when I haven't been very loveable."

"I love you, Doris, no matter what." He held up an arm and smirked at her. "Now, snuggle up close, baby. We're engaged and we can do that sort of thing, you know."

She laughed but pressed nearer to his side and rested her head against his chest. "I think this should be known as the Christmas Eve full of miracles and snow."

"And sleigh bells," Jess said as the horses trotted across the pasture back toward his place. "Just listen to those sleigh bells ring, bringing hope and cheer, and the promise of love."

Recipe

Chocolate Fudge and Mint Cookies

1 chocolate fudge cake mix (18.25 ounce)
1/2 cup butter, melted
1 teaspoon vanilla
2 eggs
1 bag Hershey's peppermint kisses
powdered sugar

Preheat oven to 350 degrees F.

Cream together eggs and butter. Add vanilla then mix in cake mix. Drop dough by rounded teaspoon onto a baking sheet. Place an unwrapped kiss in the center of each cookie.

Bake about 6-8 minutes until cookies are just set but not cooked through. Remove from oven and leave on pan until cool. Dust with powdered sugar and enjoy!

This recipe will make approximately 70 mini cookies or about 30 regular-sized cookies.

Author's Note

Thank you for coming along on another adventure to Romance, Oregon. Even as I wrote <u>Blown Into Romance</u> creating Blayne and Brooke's happily-ever-after, the thought that Doris needed a happy ending kept niggling the back of my mind.

When a group of us from the <u>Welcome to Romance</u> collection decided to write a *Christmas in Romance* series, my thoughts kept circling back around to Doris and her neighbor Jess Milne.

Just because a couple is older, doesn't mean they can't experience the same feelings they might have when they were younger.

You might have noticed at the beginning of the book, I dedicated this story to my parents. They are getting close to celebrating seventy years of marriage. Talk about true and lasting love. Around the time of their anniversary I heard on the radio about a couple who'd just celebrated their 80th anniversary. I told Dad he had a new goal to shoot for.

Joking aside, though, I love to see older

couples in love. It just makes me smile and warms my heart. So thank you to all of those who have given great examples of love lasting through the years... and those who've found love a second time around in their golden years.

I'm also giving a shout-out to Judy E. for naming Pigtails! Thank you, Judy, for the name and inspiration for a fun little character! She fit right in with all the other piggies running around the Rockin' G Ranch.

A few little tidbits of inspiration I want to share include the car Jess drove to pick up Julia for his first date. My dad has a gorgeous old 1959 Chevy he sometimes drives in parades, or just for fun. Although it isn't a coupe, the turquoise color inspired my vision of Jess driving his dad's car to pick up Julia.

We had a 4320 John Deere four-wheel drive tractor on the farm when I was growing up and I thought it would be fun to mention it as something that reminds Blayne of his grandfather because the mere sight of one makes me think of fun times spent with my dad. According to Dad, he bought the tractor at an auction at such a low price, a John Deere salesman later told him he practically stole the tractor.

And like Janet riding with Jess in the swather, I often spent my summer days with dad when I was small enough to curl up on the floor of the swather on a blanket with a supply of candy and a doll or a book.

I hope you enjoyed this sweet holiday story and I hope, too, that you'll read the other five books in this series.

Melanie D. Snitker wrote A Merry Miracle in Romance, book 2, and a little excerpt is included in this book. Be sure to check it out!

For more details about the visuals that inspired this story, be sure to visit my Pinterest board:

https://www.pinterest.com/shannahatfield/books-sleigh-bells-ring/

As always, thank you for coming along on a reading adventure with me.

Wishing you and yours a beautiful holiday season full of love!

A Merry Miracle
IN ROMANCE

BY MELANIE D. SNITKER

An excerpt...

The moment Baxter Reid pushed the door open, the scent of cookies, cupcakes, and coffee hit him hard. He breathed in deep. Though he wasn't one who normally went for fancy coffee, someone told him they made an incredible peppermint hot chocolate here. Everyone had their weakness, and for Baxter, it was peppermint.

He got in line and took in the variety of cookies and pastries in the display cabinet as he slowly made his way closer to the counter. When there were only two people in line in front of him, the sound of a voice jerked his attention to the register. He'd know that voice anywhere.

Sure enough, there stood Savannah. He chuckled and shook his head at the irony. He'd teased the girl mercilessly growing up, and they'd had many an argument yelled over the common fence between his grandparents' house and hers. Truthfully, he'd missed their banters when his family moved to Salem and he no longer visited his grandparents regularly like he used to.

He'd just moved back to Romance. Partly because he missed the small-town atmosphere and partly because he missed his grandparents. A lot of it had to do with breaking a cycle of somehow dating all the wrong women. Okay, and maybe a little of it was because he was curious how the girl next door had turned out.

Savannah hadn't noticed him yet, giving Baxter a few minutes to watch. She still had the same gorgeous black hair and eyes like pools of dark chocolate. She'd never been a petite girl, but even then, her little girl figure had been replaced with womanly curves. Savannah smiled brightly at something her customer said. It was a smile he'd often wished he could elicit from her instead of the constant look of annoyance he normally received.

He thought about all the ways he would try to aggravate her and wished he could go back in time and slap himself. If he could give his younger self some advice, it'd be that the way to make the cute girl next door notice him wasn't to annoy her ruthlessly.

The woman in front of him stepped to the side, making way for Baxter to approach the counter.

"I'll be right with you." Savannah spoke over her shoulder as she slipped a muffin into a paper bag. As soon as she handed it to her customer, she turned back with a smile on her face. The moment she recognized him, her smile faltered. "Baxter."

Her disappointment shouldn't have bothered him as much as it did. "Hey, Savannah. I didn't realize you worked here."

"I have been for about five years now." She shrugged. "So what can I get for you?"

"Someone recommended the peppermint hot chocolate, so I thought I'd give it a try." When she didn't respond, he added, "Please."

"Sure." She quoted him a price. He paid with a five and then dropped the change into the jar on the counter.

Without another word, Savannah got started on the drink, and Baxter moved out of the way so the next customer could approach the counter.

She was methodical as she worked, as though she'd memorized every step and probably never deviated from the exact order of things. That sounded like Savannah.

How many times had he teased her about being the over-careful goodie-goodie when they were kids? All of that time goading her had been a lot of fun, but looking back, he realized he might have gone a little too far. Especially if the less-than-enthusiastic way in which she greeted him was any indication.

Baxter had a huge crush on her back in the day. He'd thought of her from time to time in the years he'd lived away from Romance. Had she thought of him at all?

"Here you go."

Baxter accepted the warm cup and took a tentative sip. The chocolate-to-mint ratio was perfect. "This is great. Thank you."

"You're welcome." She hesitated as though she might ask him something. She covered it by picking up a napkin and handing it to him. "Enjoy the drink and have a great day."

"Yeah. You, too." Baxter watched as she turned to help the next customer. Banking the many questions he had about what she'd been up to in the last eight years, he left the pastry shop and stepped onto the sidewalk.

The biting cold air hit him immediately, and he was glad to have the warm cup of liquid in his hands. The temperatures had hovered a few degrees above freezing for several days. Thankfully, it should warm up a little tomorrow. Baxter had never been a huge fan of winter weather, so the less snow and ice, the better.

Although he wasn't sure which was colder: The temperatures outside, or the shoulder Savannah had given him.

The hot chocolate was enough to return to the pastry shop, but he probably would go back again even if he hated it…

*Order your copy of **A Merry Miracle** in Romance today!*

SIX SWEET NOVELLAS SURE TO WARM YOUR HEART
AVAILABLE ON AMAZON

Celebrate Christmas in Romance

Welcome to Romance — an Oregon town where love lingers around every corner and residents pull out all the stops for Christmas in Romance.

Between odd animals, lost loves, second chances, hidden identities, a secret Santa, and bickering senior citizens, it might just take a miracle to bring everyone a happily-ever-after for the holidays.

Settle in a chair by the fire, sip a cup of hot cocoa, and immerse yourself in the friendly town of Romance with this series of six sweet Christmas novellas from bestselling and award-winning authors.

Sleigh Bells Ring in Romance by Shanna Hatfield - A determined widow and a persistent rancher need a nudge toward love.

A Merry Miracle in Romance by Melanie D. Snitker - It'll take a Christmas miracle to turn a grudging friendship into true love.

Holding Onto Love in Romance by Liwen Y. Ho - A small town inn owner and a big time pop star need a reason to keep holding onto love.

A Reel Christmas in Romance by J. J. DiBenedetto - Unwittingly engaged in the plot of a classic Hollywood romance, can two email pen-pals find their way to a happy ending?

A Christmas Carol in Romance by Franky A. Brown - A bitter-on-love radio DJ and his girlfriend of romance past need a second chance.

Santa's Visit in Romance by Jessica L. Elliott - Santa's got his work cut out for him to help a reluctant couple find love during the holidays.

Find out more about Romance, Oregon on Facebook:
https://www.facebook.com/welcometoromance

Don't miss out on the other
Welcome to Romance stories!

A STORM MAY HAVE BLOWN HER INTO ROMANCE, BUT WILL A HANDSOME RANCHER AND FIVE ADORABLE PIGS GIVE HER A REASON TO STAY?.

BY *USA TODAY* BESTSELLING AUTHOR
SHANNA HATFIELD

Blown Into Romance — Artist Brooke Roberts spent her life without roots, wandering from town to town. When she seeks refuge from a freak storm in the town of Romance, she decides to stay and open a blown glass studio. Determined to immerse herself in the community, she adopts a family of pigs. Brooke is unprepared for the chaos and comfort they bring to her world, or the dashing cowboy who rescues her heart.

Solid, dependable Blayne Grundy runs a busy ranch, volunteers on various committees, and takes in stray animals too large to stay at the local animal rescue. Then a chance encounter with a beautiful, beguiling woman leaves him so befuddled, he can barely remember his own name. His predictable organized life is about to be blown away by free-spirited Brooke.

A sweet, lighthearted novella, Blown Into Romance highlights the mighty power of love and letting go.

Check out the entire
Welcome to Romance series!

Finding Forever in Romance by Melanie D. Snitker
Lost in Romance by Stacy Claflin
At Second Glance by Raine English
Blown Into Romance by Shanna Hatfield
Wired for Romance by Franky A. Brown
Restoring Romance by Tamie Dearen
Finding Dori by J.J. DeBenedetto
Katie's Chance for Romance by Jessica L. Elliott
Chasing Romance by Liwen Y. Ho
Lessons in Romance by Kit Morgan
What Happened to Romance by Franky A. Brown
Operation Romance by Jessica L. Elliott
Romantically Ever After by Liwen Y. Ho

Hopeless romantic Shanna Hatfield spent ten years as a newspaper journalist before moving into the field of marketing and public relations. Sharing the romantic stories she dreams up in her head is a perfect outlet for her love of writing, reading, and creativity. She and her husband, lovingly referred to as Captain Cavedweller, reside in the Pacific Northwest.

Shanna loves to hear from readers. Connect with her online:
Blog: shannahatfield.com
Facebook: Shanna Hatfield's Page
Shanna Hatfield's Hopeless Romantics Group
Pinterest: Shanna Hatfield
Email: shanna@shannahatfield.com

Made in the
USA
Middletown, DE

74047305R00093